A COMPETENT WITNESS

GEORGIANA YOKE AND THE

TRIAL OF H. H. HOLMES

JUDITH NICKELS

ISBN: 1497381924
ISBN 13: 9781497381926

To My Parents

"We are never deceived; we deceive ourselves."
--Goethe

1

CHICAGO

Spring 1892 – Fall 1893

NOW EVERYONE IN Chicago felt popular.

It was official. The World's Fair was set to open in the summer of 1893, and soon Chicagoans were hearing from long forgotten friends and relations, plus some fresh ones they never even knew they had before.

So Isaac Toner, with a comfortable apartment in the heart of the city, wasn't surprised, late in the spring of 1892, to receive a letter from his schoolteacher niece in Columbus, Indiana. But he was startled when he opened it. This wasn't just another bid for a future World's Fair visit. Georgiana Yoke proposed letting her move in with him, for at least a year, as soon as her current term ended.

"My work here pays very little, and my expenses are higher than we thought. It's pretty difficult to put anything by. I can use this summer to try for a better job there before the rest of the world shows up, and be all set when the Fair opens. I can pay rent to you, instead of a landlady here, and keep it in the family," making it seem reasonable, even thrifty, to walk away from her perfectly good teaching job.

Isaac considered the offer. He liked Georgiana's company. She was a lively, intelligent girl. He could use a little modest rent money. His job took him to Ohio quite often, so it might be a good thing to have his place occupied while he was away.

Poor girl, he could just imagine her writing this letter, from some pokey room in a boarding house, starved for the color and variety of city life. He could easily remember that youthful restlessness. And if he didn't rent her a room, where else might she go? Far better, since she sounded determined to come anyway, to live with family. He sent her his blessing.

"Let me know when to expect you, and I'll have the extra bedroom set up. You're wise to come early. By this time next year there won't be a room available within ten miles of downtown!"

Objections to this plan swiftly arrowed in from all sides.

"That filthy city! Really, Miss Yoke, you surprise me," said Mr. Kollmeier. Seated across the table from her in the teacher's workroom as they graded their student's exercise books, he scratched his chin through his beard with the end of his pencil, and gazed over his glasses at her. "Someone as smart as you are, caught up in all this hubbub."

"It's only going to be the greatest Exhibition the world has ever seen," Georgiana replied. "Greater than the ones they had in Paris, or London. Everyone says so."

"There's a big difference between saying and doing."

"Oh, they'll do it, all right," she said, and she reached into her teacher's satchel and pulled out a handful of newspaper clippings. "Look here. They already have commitments from every state, and pretty well every country on the globe, to have their own exhibit buildings. It's going to be huge! Think of all you could learn, all that art, and history, geography, and the different languages, and everything. You are the one to surprise me, Mr. Kollmeier. I think, as teachers, we have a duty to the students and the school to try and go."

"I was in Chicago once, and that was enough. Unfit water, and pickpockets, and the smell from those stockyards, terrible! And just think of the crowds."

Georgiana sighed. At one time she held out some mild hopes for this fellow, since he was pleasant, and nice looking, and unattached. But his placid contentment, his lack of curiosity or adventure, which another woman might find comforting, would have quickly turned her into an irritated shrew. Before the end of the first term, she had mentally moved him from potential beau to friend and confidante, and he was never the wiser about his change of status.

"The reason they'll have crowds is that everyone wants to go, and I'm sure the men planning the whole thing will think out all the problems. They're building new train lines and roads, and plumbing. They're draining the marshes to build lagoons, and when it's done they're going to light them all up at night, so it will look just like Venice! Really, since neither of us are likely to ever get to Europe, why not go to the next best thing?"

Mr. Kollmeier smiled. "*Mid pleasures and palaces though we may roam; Be it ever so humble, there's no place like home*," he quoted. Georgiana made a black checkmark, pressing her pencil so hard it almost made a hole in the paper.

"No interest in science? The new things they're doing with electricity? What about the engineering? There's this man, named Ferris, building a great iron wheel more complicated than the Eiffel Tower, and when it's done you'll be able to get in a car and ride to the top, higher than a bird. Think about that!"

"You wouldn't be afraid?"

"No, I wouldn't," she said, though as a daughter of the flat Midwest, Georgiana had no real experience of heights. "I think I'd love it."

Mr. Kollmeier finished his last correction, and stacked his papers neatly in his case.

"I understand your feelings, but really, I think you should just plan to visit for a week or two. No more. I would hate to see you give up your job here. And I'm sure your mother will agree with me."

He wished her good night, and left her with her work, and this time her pencil finally did pierce a page of her student's workbook.

Mr. Kollmeier correctly predicted her mother's reaction.

"What about your education?" Mary Yoke protested in her letter, when she first heard the news. After all, it was she who sacrificed to pay for teacher's college. The fact that her brother was making this misadventure possible just added to her sense of helpless outrage. *"You worked so hard to get this job!"*

"Mother, you worry far too much. They have schools in Chicago, you know," Georgiana wrote back in a breezy reply, though she didn't actually say she intended to apply for another teaching job.

Her godfather and uncle, Nelson Yoke, expressed other concerns.

"It's a big city, and Isaac is the only one you know there. I worry about your safety, as I know your father would. I'd be much happier if you had a companion with you," he wrote. She was ready for that one, and shot back an answer the same day.

"Central Normal College is renting a house, right by Lake Michigan, for a reunion of students attending the Fair," and she included a clipping about it from her alumni newspaper as proof. *"Plenty of them are already heading to Chicago. There will be so many people I know from Danville, I'll very likely be tripping all over them!"*

At the end of the term, Georgiana took the train from Columbus to her childhood home, the nearby town of Edinburgh, Indiana, to pay a farewell visit to some relatives, and even there, she couldn't escape disapproval. Jacob Toner, her mother's elderly cousin, wondered at her foolishness.

"Why are you so restless nowadays? Why can't you just stay put?"

His health was failing, and since the weather was mild, she volunteered to push his wheeled chair outside. Now, as they took a rest in front of the shops on Main Cross Street, Georgiana leaned back for a moment against a storefront wall made warm by the sun. A pattern of arched bricks topped the second story windows across the street, like a long row of raised eyebrows, skeptically awaiting an explanation for this folly.

"When you first came to Edinburgh," she said, "there was almost nothing here. You built the mill, and the town grew up around it, but now it's all done. Every generation wants to make something new for itself, just as you did."

"Some of the boys from your high school class work at the mill, and they don't seem to mind it."

"I know, but they still might want to go to the Fair. To see everything that's coming, bring ideas back with them, improvements. I guess before long we'll see telephone wires strung right down this street," she said, and the old man answered with a snort.

"Telephones! In Edinburgh! What a stupid waste of money!"

"Why couldn't you renew your contract, go to Chicago, and if you can't find a job this summer, just come back to Columbus in the fall?" Mary pleaded a month later, even as she helped Georgiana pack. Her arms loaded with clothes to be folded, she surveyed the pile on the bed they must somehow fit into the trunk for Chicago.

"Mother, I can't believe you would suggest something so dishonest! Anyway, I've already given my notice, and you know they need time to find another teacher," and with that, Mary was shamed into uneasy silence, and Georgiana got her way.

MARY DIDN'T HAVE to worry. Georgiana found employment within a week after Uncle Isaac met her at the station. Chicago was getting ready for the Fair by expanding everything it had, and to run the new hotels, restaurants, trains, trolleys and shops, it preferred the ambitious, energetic young workers supplied by the nation's small towns.

She had always intended to apply at one of the great department stores. She wanted to try first at Marshall Field's, but Isaac said, "Do you know anyone there? I hear it's a hard place to get into without a connection."

From the sitting room of his third floor walkup, Georgiana surveyed the busy length of State Street.

"What about that one?" She pointed to the massive new Siegel Cooper store on the opposite side, and as it happened, Uncle Isaac did have a friend of a friend there.

THE JOB WAS hers even before she sat down in the chair the two young men hurried to hold for her. Georgiana Yoke was exactly the type they liked to put on the selling floor. Pretty as a china doll, fair complexion, blond hair, and big blue eyes. Posture straight against the back of her chair, hands folded demurely in her lap. Pleasing voice, educated diction, college diploma, two years teaching experience. Character reference from the Methodist minister back in Indiana. Respectable beyond a doubt, as she earnestly explained that while she was willing to work in almost any department, she could never agree to sell alcohol. They assured her only men worked in the sales of wine and spirits.

After Georgiana departed, employment agreement in hand, one of them whistled at the closed door.

"That little missy could sell cages to lions!"

"What do you call that stone, they use in the Indian jewelry?" the other man said. He'd been almost startled by the unusual color of Miss Yoke's enormous eyes.

"You mean turquoise?"

"Right. That's the stuff. Did you notice her eyes? I've never seen any like that."

"The problem with good lookers, we get 'em trained up and next thing you know they're engaged. I bet you a dollar she's gone in a year."

"Our location cannot be better," Georgiana wrote reassuringly to Mary. *"My job is on the southeast corner of State and Van Buren Streets, and Uncle Isaac's apartment is on the northwest corner. I can leave work on a street full of people at any time of the day or night, and be home in less than five minutes.*

"Our Methodist Church is just a seven-block walk, and Mother, you will be shocked to learn what that building is like. The Church owns the prop-erty, a four-story building, and the bottom two are stores and offices, with the Church itself on the upper floors! They call it the Methodist Corner, the oldest church in the city. Don't worry, on the Sabbath we have it all to ourselves, but during the week, the rents make a nice income for the missions and everything they do. They are very practical here in Chicago!"

She saw no reason to add that a brewery occupied the lower level of Uncle Isaac's building. Nor did she mention how often Uncle Isaac traveled on business, so much of the time she would be living alone.

In their cheery letters back to Mary in Franklin, Indiana, Georgiana and Isaac engaged in an unspoken agreement of omission.

The two men in the Hiring department drew lots to see which of them would take Georgiana for the customary tour of the store on her first morning of work, but as it happened, there were five people starting that Monday morning, three other women and one

man, so both of them got to go. They met the group of new workers in the basement level cloakroom, made introductions, then led
the way upstairs.

Georgiana marveled with the others at the magnificence of
the handsome new building, with its lofty, ornate ceilings, freshly
waxed wood floors, vibrant colors and inviting textures of all the
splendid goods, gleaming beneath rows of electric globes.

The interior, her guides explained, was a miracle of modern
technology. The lower floors would stay pleasantly cool all summer, due to an elaborate system of air chilled by water passed over
huge ice blocks and fanned throughout the building. In winter, massive coal furnaces pumped heated air through radiators in the floor,
keeping them toasty warm even when the temperatures outside fell
below zero. They observed the operation of the store's own switchboard, staffed by girls briskly plugging and unplugging switches
into the twelve telephone lines already installed, with more on the
way.

Georgiana was the only one of the group who had never ridden
in an elevator, but she said nothing as they filed in and a smiling,
uniformed operator banged together the trellis-patterned wrought
iron doors, turned a crank and transported them, in just moments,
from the ground floor all the way to the top of the building, eight
stories up, causing an unexpectedly pleasurable swoop deep down
in her stomach.

Emerging from the elevator, she dared herself to walk right to a
grand window nearly thrice her height, lean her head out the opening and stare straight down at the sidewalk, past first floor awnings
to the tops of hats bobbing by, propelled by striding trousers and
billowing hem-kicked skirts. By turning her gaze from the right to
the left she could scan the entire brick lined gorge of State Street.
Across the street and one block north, past the elevated rail tracks
under construction, she spotted her uncle's apartment window,
five stories below.

"This is mighty exciting for a prairie girl," she said, smiling at her guides as she pulled her head back in.

It took the better part of the morning to visit more than fifty departments, and even then they didn't see them all. How long would her next letter to her mother have to be, she wondered, to describe all this grandeur, this novelty, all this *fun*? What would astonish Mary the most?

Perhaps the Stationery department, designed to look like a library, where a customer could sample any of hundreds of notepapers by sitting at a fine writing desk and doing all her morning correspondence, which the staff would obligingly mail for her. One could practice her most elegant handwriting using fountain pens, miniature marble sculptures as beautiful as any jewelry, cleverly devised to contain their own inkwells.

Or Needlework, with its array of fabrics, ribbons, yarns, threads, and patterns for every imaginable project, more colorful than any garden. The women who staffed the area not only sold the merchandise, but were also expert in using it, providing impromptu lessons in sewing, knitting and fancy embroidery to customers throughout the day.

They peeked in at a hair salon, and then for a special treat they sampled one of the dozen different teas available in the cheery teashop, and dainty cut sandwiches served on delicately patterned little platters.

Georgiana counted dozens of racks of ready-to-wear clothing for women, for men, even some for children. She ran her hand over lightweight walking coats, lace collars, soft kid gloves and long fringed silk scarves. She held up high heel leather shoes. She studied women's hats in every possible color, fabric and shape, topped with feathers, with flowers, with fruit.

Next came furniture, chintz draperies, Oriental rugs, cut glass lamps, tall vases and elaborate statuary, many brought in from overseas, the guides explained, as interest in foreign goods was expected to rise with the coming of the World's Fair. The store imported gourmet foods, too, chocolate and cocoanut, raisins and figs, spices from every corner of the world. For educated buyers, there were long sets of leather-bound encyclopedias, and dictionaries on a stand, colorful globes, framed maps, and telescopes. And toys, such as she never dreamed of when she was a child, beautiful German bisque-head dolls in traditional folk costumes, kaleidoscopes, music boxes and mechanical trains, hoops and bicycles.

"These playthings on display in the summer are only a sample," one of the men told the group. "In December, the Toy section expands, it will cover this whole floor area. Better be ready — Christmas is quite a busy time!"

Towards the end of the morning, sensing the ladies might be tiring, the men waited in the corridor while Georgiana and the other women toured the Ladies' Lounge. This room, of course, was reserved for customers, but on this one special occasion, new employees were allowed to visit, and be amazed.

Pure white tiles ran across the floors and all the way up the walls to the vaulted ceiling. Hot and cold water flowed through twin faucets into deep white marble sinks. Uniformed attendants, also in white, courteous as ladies' maids, waited to see to every need: to loosen tightly laced garments, hand out warm towels, fetch ice water, and provide everything from talcum powder to needles and thread. Wide, upholstered chairs with matching tasseled ottomans invited exhausted shoppers to remove their shoes and gather their strength. Full length, gilt-framed mirrors with lights on the sides and above allowed women to arrange their hair, hats, and bustles to perfection before venturing back out to shop some more.

What incredible convenience! With such a facility available to her, a woman might be away from home for three hours, or five, or even the whole day, and never have to worry about her comfort.

When they returned to the elevator, one of the guides told the operator, "Let us out at the second floor," and with that they reached the finale of their tour.

A grand staircase led to the first floor rotunda, the largest, most open selling area, and midway down, a wide balcony with an intricately carved iron railing overlooked the whole expanse. A row of bright electric chandelier lights graced the high ceiling, and from glass-topped counters and mirrored shelves all varieties of the most luxurious wares gleamed up at them: sets of crystal glassware and floral patterned sets of dishes, silver trays and teapots, glass perfume bottles. From this vantage they heard the steady hum of commerce below, of clerks and customers in polite exchange, the patter of cash boys running for change and receipts, occasional excited voices and laughter of women and the swish of their petticoats and skirts like a hundred stiff bristle brooms sweeping over the polished floor.

"During the Christmas season, we perform choral music from this balcony," the man said. "The customers are delighted by it. There's a children's choir, as well as other musical groups from among the staff. I myself sing tenor with the men's quartet. If any of you are interested in joining, we can sign you up for an audition," and he looked hopefully at Georgiana, who shook her head. She sang heartily in the safety a whole congregation, but that was all.

They shook hands all around, and thanked the men for the tour, and expressed how happy they all were to be working in such a fine store. They were directed to the lunchroom, and given their assignments for the afternoon. The man was sent to the upper offices; he was a new assistant in Accounting. The other women were all new clerks, like Georgiana, but each of them had some previous selling experience, so they were sent to more expensive departments. Perfume. Luggage. Coats.

Georgiana joined them in the crowded lunchroom, then made her way to her new home in Handkerchiefs.

"We stock over four hundred different types of handkerchiefs, Miss Yoke," said the earnest young supervisor who undertook her training.

"My goodness," she said. "You must really have to study to keep track of them all," and he flushed a little.

"This side for men, the other for ladies, starting here, the cheapest at ten cents each, but they go for seven and a half cents during the Leader Bankrupt Sale. That will be in the newspapers on our bargain days. An advance copy of our advertisements will be provided to you each morning."

"What's there?" she said, pointing to a locked glass case. A key ring emerged from inside his waistcoat, and he opened the door and brought out a handful of neatly folded, delicate white wisps of fabric.

"Our very best stock, silk lace, can run up to five dollars, depending on the quality, workmanship, weight and source of the fabric. Imported ones here, Irish lace, the most expensive, you see," and she nodded as he replaced them.

"Locked, of course, because of thieves. You must be on the lookout, always, though you must never confront a suspicious customer yourself. Call a cash boy to get a manager if you suspect someone pilfering the merchandise. A constant problem, especially in this department, for naturally, the same thing that makes a handkerchief an excellent gift also makes it vulnerable to theft."

He took his own out from his pocket, and wiped his forehead. Extended speeches were not his strength, but something about this attractive new clerk made him want to exert himself. He stood up a little straighter.

"I can see that," she said. Encouraged, the handkerchief in his hand waved about like a flag.

"Indeed, what else could fulfill the need so perfectly? There's a handkerchief made for every price, every occasion. Not much chance of choosing the wrong one by mistake. They're portable, lightweight, cheap to post, simple to wrap in tissue. Everyone needs them. They must often be replaced. We do an astounding volume of business, Miss Yoke," and for his efforts he earned a smile so charming, he would have bought a dozen handkerchiefs from her right then, had he been a customer.

"I shall do my very best to increase sales further," she said.

"I am sure of it. I have no doubt whatever. You will do well, and learn fast. Then, of course, before you know it, the holidays will be upon us." He rolled his eyes. "And I will be frank with you, Miss Yoke. Christmastime, in the Handkerchief department, is madness!"

He made introductions and left her to her two new coworkers, Tillie and Nettie. She guessed they were about thirty years old. Tillie was slight and Nettie was stout, but they both wore the same pinched lines about the mouth and the forehead. During a mid-afternoon lull in business, the three of them gathered a pile of loose handkerchiefs scattered about the display counter, and Georgiana got a lesson in the proper way to fold them.

"Have you worked in a store before, Georgiana?" Nettie asked. Female colleagues dispensed with formality and went straight to first names.

"No," she said, "I know I have a lot to learn."

"So this is your first job?"

Georgiana hesitated. She had blundered, her first week of teaching school in Columbus. She sailed in, fresh from college, and explained to her older, more experienced colleagues everything they were doing wrong. No more corporal punishment. No more rote memorization of long lists of facts. Teachers must be more like a friend than a master in the new methods of today, she informed them, oblivious to their silent anger.

It took weeks to undo the damage, and she was actually relieved when her contract was renewed for the second year, but some of the teachers never fully forgave or trusted her. She wasn't about to make the same mistake twice.

"I helped out at a school for a while, but the pay was really low. I just wanted to get to Chicago in time for the Fair," she replied. "I'm ready to help all I can, I hope you'll teach me what I need to know." She said nothing about attending college. She had learned in her interview that she would be one of the few store clerks with any higher education.

Nettie relented. This new girl might not be so bad, even if she did seem a little stuck up at first.

"Well of course, there *is* a lot. The main thing is to know the rules, early on. You don't want to learn them the hard way!"

"We get an employee newsletter, and when they make up a new rule, it's sure to be in it. Usually if a customer complains about something," Tillie said. "But to start with, never chew gum. Or your nails."

Georgiana nodded. She never did either of those things. She held up a delicate square of fabric, to make sure the embroidery showed on the outside when she folded it.

"Never sit on the counter. In fact, you can't sit down at all, except at lunch."

"Most of us keep an extra pair of shoes here, one size larger," Nettie said. She bent over and pulled her own out from below the display case to show Georgiana. "You'll be glad of it by the end of the day, especially at the holidays. Have you heard about Christmas?"

"Well, it seems very festive, with the music and everything," Georgiana said, and the two women smirked at each other.

"That's almost funny." Nettie looked around to make sure no supervisor was in sight, then went ahead and slipped off her shoes and put the bigger ones on.

"You won't believe how long they make you work, and no overtime pay," Tillie said. "You get a voucher for dinner, that's all. And don't even think of taking time off. Everyone works right up until

Christmas day. No chance to visit your family. Where are you from, Georgiana?"

"Indiana," she replied, "a small town near Indianapolis."

"I'm from Wisconsin," Tillie said, "and I haven't seen my family in three years. No time."

"Never wear jewelry, not even a ring," Nettie said, looking closely at Georgiana's ears for signs of a piercing. There were none, but she noticed Georgiana frown a little at this last restriction. "And watch out for the Jewelry department girls, they have a reputation for being fast."

"Not all of them, Nettie!" Tillie protested, and Georgiana decided Tillie was the kinder of the two. "Some of them are all right."

"We like all the girls in Hats," Nettie said. "Gloves are pretty nice too. Don't even try to be friends with Furs. They're all snobby, because they sell with men, on commission."

"Commission? What's that?"

"Don't you know what that is? You are a green one! That means you're paid on what you sell, instead of wages like us. That's where the money is. A few women are rich from commissions, like Mrs. Margarite." With the mention of the legendary saleswoman, the two veterans were silent for a moment, and then Nettie explained.

"She's the queen of Corsets. She has such a following of customers! I heard she sent out twelve hundred Christmas cards last year. Women bring in their daughters, and their granddaughters, just to be fitted by her. They say she can take two inches off anyone's waist, just like magic. Management can't touch her, she makes her own hours, does just what she wants, because if she ever left for another store, she'd take all her customers along with her. They offered to make her a buyer, but she turned it down, she makes so much more money selling!"

The three women were silent again for a while, folding steadily but not too fast, so they wouldn't run out of handkerchiefs and appear idle. Then Nettie returned to store rules.

"Don't talk to union men. In fact, make it a point never to be seen with them at all, even outside of work, because someone might spy on you and report it to management. They take no chances with union people."

"As much as the union men," Tillie added, "watch out for the Lady Bountifuls."

"Lady Bountifuls?"

"Church women, or from the settlement houses like Hull, checking up on working conditions. 'How long to do have to stand?' 'What do they pay you?' 'Are you docked if you get sick?' They come right up while you're trying to wait on customers, and ask you all these questions, as if it's any of their business!"

Georgiana wondered how Nettie and Tillie could complain about being overworked at Christmas, yet be so resentful of anyone trying to improve their lot. Pride, she supposed. It must seem like taking charity. At the Methodist Corner, a Women's Committee regularly visited stores and factories asking exactly those kinds of questions, to protect working girls and keep them from falling into evil.

"Maybe they mean well, but of course they can't change any-thing. The store can do whatever it wants," she said. It seemed to be the right answer, because Nettie and Tillie smiled at her, and she felt proud of herself for her newfound diplomacy. A woman customer approached the counter, and they proceeded to show Georgiana the right way to sell a handkerchief.

Later, when it seemed safe to leave Georgiana on her own for a few minutes, Nettie and Tillie headed to the restroom reserved for female employees, far down a dank corridor in the basement, a very different kind of facility than the clean, bright Ladies' Lounge that Georgiana toured earlier in the day.

"So, what do you think of the new girl?" Nettie said.

"She seems all right."

"One of the boys in Hiring told me he made a bet she won't last a year, someone will snatch her away."

"Well, she *is* pretty. He could be right."

"I think she won't last a year," Nettie said. "But not because she'll get engaged. I don't think she has the right mental attitude."

"What do you mean? She seems very eager to me."

"She's eager, yes, but not for work. She may do this for a while, but deep down, she doesn't really think of herself as a clerk. She thinks she's a customer."

The prospect of those long hours on her feet worried Georgiana, because she had a secret. She suffered from a longstanding medical condition that caused occasional dizziness and shortness of breath, especially when she was tired. Keeping this job, of course, meant she must conceal her weakness.

To control these symptoms, on her doctor's orders, Georgiana followed a specialized diet rich in iodine. In addition to forcing herself to eat tinned oysters and clams, she had to sprinkle dried kelp on all her other food. She found it easier to do this discreetly, and cheaper as well, if she avoided lunch counters and carried in her own meals from home to the staff lunchroom.

By the end of the summer Georgiana was in the habit of sharing a table with several other employees who also economized in this way. Her favorite companion was a young woman from the Sewing department, Mary Ellen Ladd.

Nettie and Tillie exchanged a disapproving frown the first time this happened. Saleswomen rarely socialized with anyone from Sewing, but Georgiana had taken a liking to the vivacious Irish girl, and insisted they make room for her.

Mary Ellen had dark curled hair and snapping brown eyes. She was as pretty, in her way, as Georgiana, but since she was already married, she wasn't interested in making friends with young men.

Mary Ellen thought it funny, though, to note how often men found a way to join them, and she had to tease Georgiana about it. The two could be eating together, deep in female conversation, when first one, then another, cash boy or clerk or even an assistant manager would find a reason to offer a passing remark, or ask a question, then suddenly a whole group pulled up chairs.

"They buzz around you like bees to the hive, Georgiana! They can't help themselves," she said, which pleased Georgiana even as she protested they did no such thing.

The management at Siegel Cooper encouraged congeniality between male and female employees as good for business, but strictly forbade romance. Employee conversations in the lunchroom were monitored to discourage bad language or flirting, so all these encounters were limited to innocent banter.

Leading the group of admirers was Harry Chapman, supervisor of the store porters, a freckled and sandy haired, pleasantly homely fellow with the wide smile and friendly cheer of a salesman. On discovering their birthdays were just two months apart, with herself the elder, Georgiana took to calling him "Little Brother," for, she explained, Johnny, her own little brother, wasn't available for her to lecture or scold, so Harry must stand in for him. While the lunchroom supervisor was deeply absorbed in his Herald Tribune, Harry protested this indignity.

"Come now, Miss Yoke," he said, gesturing at the assembled group with his sandwich. "Look at all these suffering minions! You take none of us seriously. You've broken a dozen hearts this week alone. What's a fellow supposed to do?"

"I'll take them seriously," she said, as Mary Ellen looked on, laughing, "when they act seriously. When I see some ambition, proportionate to the opportunities of this great city. Now really, what do I see here before me? Shirkers, one and all!"

"How can you say that, when we were here last night until nearly eleven? All you females leave before it's dark, how can you know how long and hard we work?"

"I heard it was nine-thirty, and then what did you do, but go to a dance hall, or a liquor saloon?"

"That charge is denied!"

"And what did you do every Sabbath this summer, but go swimming in that ice cold lake! Who could take seriously anyone who does that?"

"Perhaps everyone was getting baptized. Did you think of that possibility?"

"Once you've been, why go back every week? Just what sort of sinners are you?"

"Actually," Harry said, "there's a purely practical method in our madness. It spares us the trouble of our Saturday night bath, you see, if we're all cleaned up by the lake on Sunday."

"Oh please," said Georgiana, tossing the back of her hand over her eyes, "don't force me to contemplate you in the bath!" and the laughter erupting around the table caught the attention of the monitor, causing him to lower the newspaper and glare, prompting shushing and elbowing from the group of jovial coworkers.

Three days before Christmas, Georgiana arrived at work to find Nettie red-eyed and pale, her pain-and-worry lines deeper than ever.

"You'll have to stay even longer than you planned, Georgiana. Tillie's gone." She used a cheap handkerchief from the stock drawer to dab her eyes.

"What's happened?"

"Her sister. She had an accident, in a factory. Some piece of something went flying. She lost an eye."

Georgiana covered her mouth in horror.

"Tillie is taking her home to Wisconsin. I don't know if she'll ever come back, after this. She's so upset. Her sister has to get a glass eye."

"Is the factory going to help her?" Georgiana asked. "Give her some compensation? Pay for her doctor, at least?"

Nettie shook her head.

"I think all she got was a one way ticket home. And she was a pretty girl, Tillie's sister."

Customers started milling through the aisles; the store had already opened while they were talking. Nettie tucked the handkerchief in the waistband of her skirt, and straightened her shoulders.

"Her life is ruined, that's all there is to it. There's nothing more to say. Best get to work. Christmas is for customers, not for us."

They put their larger shoes on early, and took turns sneaking sips of water and peppermints to keep their strength up through the hectic extended shopping hours. When the supervisor finally dropped by to check on them, it was nearly five o'clock, and neither girl had a lunch break yet. Georgiana declared every person in Chicago must be suffering from a head cold, they bought so many handkerchiefs, and he nodded his approval but didn't offer any sympathy or help, just handed out their dinner vouchers and hoped they could find a chance to use them.

They didn't have any time to enjoy the festive decorations, or return merry holiday greetings. They never heard the chorus of sweet, familiar carols swelling from the balcony over the great sparkling sales floor.

Georgiana was far too busy to remember the quiet, well-dressed man who purchased gifts of fine Irish lace handkerchiefs for all the typewriter girls in his office.

But he remembered her.

WHEN HE RETURNED in early March to order special quality, monogrammed handkerchiefs for himself, he thanked her for the excellent service previously received. She was flattered and pleased. Between the complainers and bargain hunters she patiently endured every day, it made a nice change to be paid a compliment.

"We're delighted your employees were happy with their gifts, sir," she said as she wrote his order. He studied a book of letter styles for the monogram.

"They should be done like this, with the letters **HH**." He spoke with the confident authority of one who is used to directing others. "Here is my card, have them sent to this address."

The card stock was stiff, the printing elegant. She read it aloud. **"Dr. Henry Holmes."**

"No relation," he said, "to either Sherlock or Oliver Wendell," and from behind his long mustache an inviting smile broke out. His teeth were perfectly straight, and very white. His blue eyes glowed with amusement at his own wit.

"I'll make sure they are sent out without delay, as soon as they're finished. I expect no later than Thursday," she said, and she smiled back at him before waiting on another customer.

The doctor turned to leave, then stopped, watching her from the other side of the counter until she was free, and then he approached her again.

"I've changed my mind. Don't have them sent. I'll come back on Thursday to pick them up," he said, and he gazed at her, quite directly, before vanishing into the crowded aisle. She looked down and noticed his card was still in her hand.

On Wednesday night, Georgiana decided to wash her hair. She usually saved that chore for closer to Sunday, but Uncle Isaac was away, so she could enjoy the luxury of a long bath. She decided it was high time to open up a pretty box of scented Pears soap that she'd been saving since Christmas.

She took her time drying her hair by the bathroom radiator, and slowly counted a hundred brush strokes to bring out the shine. While she was at it, she ran a buffing stick over her fingernails. Then, for no particular reason, she pressed a new shirtwaist, a crisp white one, the only color other than black acceptable to wear on the selling floor.

On Thursday morning, she checked the special order drawer, and the doctor's handkerchiefs were ready. They were still there when she left for her lunch break. By three o'clock she decided she was silly, anticipating another conversation with this man who, after all, was just a customer, and had done nothing more than act pleasant and polite.

At a quarter to five she saw him, engaged in a lively conversation with a girl she knew slightly from the Jewelry department. The girl looked up at his face, laughing and talking in great high spirits. They strolled, slowly, along the aisle and then up to her counter.

"Miss Yoke," the girl said. "May I present my neighbor, Dr. Holmes? Dr. Holmes, this is Miss Yoke," and then, duty done, she bounced away with a saucy backward grin.

"It's a pleasure to meet you, Miss Yoke," he said, as cordially as if this was a social occasion. "Have you sold many handkerchiefs today?"

He set his walking stick against the counter, and took his time finding his merchandise ticket, ignoring the other customers now waiting in line behind him.

"Business is going very well, thank you," she replied, "and thank you for shopping with us." She gave him her most winning, professional smile along with his parcel, and perhaps it was only her imagination, but it seemed when he took it as if he deliberately brushed his hand against hers.

The Jewelry girl pounced the next morning.

"He's sweet on you!" she declared, which disturbed Georgiana's sense of propriety. She remembered Nettie's warning about the Jewelry department.

"He's probably just friendly to all the sales girls," she said.

"No, really," the girl insisted. "He made a point of seeking me out, just to be introduced to you. He's quite the catch, Georgiana, he's got a building that takes up a whole block; in our neighborhood they call it the Castle. When the Fair starts, he'll have dozens of tenants there, paying top dollar to be near the train. My father says he's a very clever businessman."

"Please don't start any rumors," Georgiana said, embarrassed, and fearful that her own fanciful thoughts might be that obvious. Now the Jewelry department girl was put off.

"Oh well," she said, "you're probably right. I've seen him bicycling around the neighborhood with another girl. Maybe he's only interested in handkerchiefs after all."

On the first Sunday in April, Georgiana and Uncle Isaac walked down the flights of stairs from church and spilled out with the crowd onto the sidewalk to shake hands with the minister. She thought for a moment she glimpsed Dr. Holmes, though she hadn't noticed him among the congregation during the service. Then, upon turning, she found herself face to face with him.

"Why, hello there, good morning Miss Yoke," he said, with a greeting so warm and familiar, she might be one of his oldest friends. He smiled expectantly at her uncle.

She introduced them, and before she knew it the three of them were walking south on State Street together. She was in the middle and the two men chatted with great animation right past her head. Apparently they had several business acquaintances in common, and each must be named and declared a fine fellow, and isn't travel getting better now with all the added trains, and will the economic recession hurt attendance at the Fair? She began to feel a bit miffed, and considered saying something pointed by the time they reached the entrance to the apartment.

"Well, it was nice to see you again, Dr. Holmes," and she held out a gloved hand. "Perhaps you'll be shopping again with us soon." Uncle Isaac likewise gave his new friend a hearty handshake.

"Perhaps I will," Dr. Holmes said, and then he gave her a special, knowing look, as if they had been sharing a private joke during the whole walk. She forgot her annoyance.

But he did not shop at the store that week. He did not attend church the following Sunday.

On Thursday evening, Uncle Isaac sorted through his mail.

"Well, now, what have we here?" he said, holding out an envelope. "Who do we know in Englewood?"

He tore it open, held out two tickets, and read the sheet.

"Why, it's from your friend, the doctor. These are for the orchestra, on Saturday night. He had to leave town, quite unexpectedly. He hates to see them go to waste, and hopes we might make use of them. What a thoughtful gesture."

Georgiana read the message, too. It was cordial yet formal, written on heavy, expensive stationary with the same DR. HENRY HOLMES engraving as the business card.

"Where is the Auditorium?"

"Oh, just a couple of blocks from here, on LaSalle and Congress streets. You may have seen it, the big building that looks like a fortress. Part of it is offices and such, but the theatre is magnificent."

Georgiana took the tickets and studied them, turning them over in her hand.

"What should we do with these?"

Uncle Isaac picked up the newspaper, and consulted the Music & Drama column.

"Why, if you've nothing else to do, we should go! The program looks very fine."

"It seems a little forward to go ahead and take them," she said. "I really don't know him very well," but Uncle Isaac dismissed her worry with a wave of the paper.

"People in the city pass around tickets all the time, it's just a part of life here, with so much entertainment going on. Really not unusual, and he's right, it would be a shame to let them go to waste."

"I wonder why he picked us, instead of any other friends," she said.

"Because we live right around the corner! He probably thought it would be the most convenient for us," and this explanation seemed to make the most sense. It would be thriftless to throw away expensive tickets, and felt churlish to give them to someone else.

She started to share some of her uncle's enthusiasm. It was quite a thing, really, to be a part of a city where people just exchanged theatre tickets like calling cards, and could stroll only a few blocks away to hear a prestigious orchestra play the world's great music. Now, only one question remained.

"What should I wear? I don't have an evening dress," and Uncle Isaac grinned at this most feminine concern.

"Well, Georgiana, I guess that's why you work in a department store."

A smart silk dress lay buried in a storeroom, a rich plum color, with restrained gigot sleeves, just a moderate puff from the shoulder, tapering to cream-colored lace over the forearms. It had ripped when someone stepped on it, torn at the waist seam as well as the hem, and the Dress department manager set it aside, forgotten, until Georgiana noticed it and calculated it was just her size. It took very little effort to convince him that since it was from last season, it wasn't worth the labor to repair it, and would be far better instead to sell it very cheaply to her.

At lunch, she nonchalantly slipped a bag containing the dress to Mary Ellen, who took it back to the Sewing department to fit in between her other jobs. At five o'clock, on the way out the door, she dropped off the wrapped parcel to the Handkerchief department.

Georgiana by then also acquired some pearl-buttoned gloves and a pretty pearl-and-lace hair ornament from Hats. She avoided the Jewelry department. She would just have to polish her boots, since there was no money left for new shoes, and anyway, the weather threatened some late season snow. She had a cream colored shawl of fine wool, knitted by Mary, not very fancy but good enough, to get her from their apartment to the performance without freezing.

The Auditorium Theatre, still quite new, was already world famous for its exquisite beauty and acoustical perfection.

"This is the very spot where the Republicans nominated President Harrison," Uncle Isaac said with obvious civic pride as he steered her by the elbow through the crowded lobby. "The designer of the building, Mr. Sullivan, everyone calls him a genius," but the atmosphere was so overwhelming she couldn't even reply. Along the wide corridor, small groups of men and women chatted and posed in magnificently carved inglenooks, perfect small spaces like life sized picture frames, designed to set off the elaborate beauty of the women's gowns.

They found their seats and she sank into hers gratefully, gazing all around and then up, enchanted by rows of electric lights sparkling down from grand arches that spanned the domed ceiling, like bright metallic rainbows cast from their own pots of gold. It was thrilling enough just to sit there and savor the work of art in which she found herself, but then the sparkles dimmed to the incandescence of stars, and the crowd hushed.

Mozart. Beethoven. Berlioz.

Georgiana had heard fine music before, at church, and at college, and the theatre in Columbus, but never anything even close to this performance. Great, brimming surges of sound, vivid and joyous, left her astonished, buoyant, like a fresh witness at the world's greatest revival.

That jubilation stayed with her on the walk home, the whole rest of the evening, and later in bed. The uplifting feeling remained, too, the next morning after church, when she emerged from the building and glanced around the crowded sidewalk, hoping for a chance to thank their benefactor. Like the previous week, however, he was not there. She guessed that meant he was still out of town, so they would have to be satisfied with sending a gracious thank you note.

A week or so later, Uncle Isaac got the chance to express their gratitude in person. At the luncheon counter nearest his office, seemingly quite by chance, he ran into Dr. Holmes, ducking in from the rain.

"Please do sit, and let me buy you a cup of coffee," he said, "and tell you how much my niece and I enjoyed the concert!"

"Well, thanks, I don't mind if I do, for a bit," and Dr. Holmes took the next seat. "I'm just trying to warm up. I certainly hope the weather cooperates for the opening," and they discussed the upcoming Fair for some time, and then Isaac returned to their first topic, the concert at the Auditorium.

"Georgiana had never been there before, what a wonderful experience for her," he told the doctor, who appeared gratified his gift was put to good use.

"She's a charming young woman, you're very lucky. Will she stay on, do you suppose, after the Fair?"

"She'd like to. I think she found home rather dull. Like all the modern girls now, she wants to be on her own a while, and who can blame them? Good for them, I say."

"Yes, up to a point, but a young girl still needs a chaperone, if only to keep track of all the suitors."

"Oh, well, yes, she has a good number of beaus, I think there's someone she always sits with in a picnic group from her work, and maybe another one at church, and with the Fair, she'll have a whole new supply of friends in town from her college. These young folks like to go out in big groups, and seem to have a great deal of fun."

Dr. Holmes set down his coffee cup.

"But did you not say you travel quite often? If I were you, I should worry a little, leaving her all on her own."

Isaac, now recalling he had an extended trip coming up, found himself feeling uncomfortably guilty. Perhaps he should have a friend check up on her while he was away? Just as this thought crossed his mind, his companion made a most generous offer.

"I would be happy to take her out for a dinner one night next week, just to make sure all is well," and after they exchanged a warm handshake and Dr. Holmes went on his way, Isaac felt very much relieved.

Thank goodness she invested in the plum silk, was all Georgiana could think, as Dr. Holmes ushered her in to the lobby of the Palmer House, the most celebrated hotel and restaurant in Chicago. Her dress was just barely fine enough for this elegant setting. Perhaps he sensed her trepidation, because he steered her away from the crowded main restaurant, where a tight bouquet of women arranged themselves in the flattering glow of a golden skylight.

Instead, he led her to a smaller, darker, more intimate dining room on the next floor. Here Dr. Holmes again showed that confident sense of command she first noticed at the store, when he overruled the headwaiter and selected the table he wanted, in a corner, out of the light, his chair facing the entrance.

Now they settled in and he took pains to make her comfortable, but her fear of making of an awkward mistake rose again with the arrival of two oversized, leather-bound, flower-adorned calligraphies of bewildering supper choices.

Hers, of course, was the ladies' menu, which omitted prices. She had been out to dinner at a restaurant in Columbus with a similar custom, but no restaurant in Columbus was so grand or costly as the Palmer House. And in Columbus, the menu was written in plain English, with items like Chicken and Dumplings, or Roast Beef with Mashed Potatoes and Gravy. What in the world was *Consomme Printaniere? Petit Boche a la Reine? Pique a la Macedoine?* Would *Glace in Brandy Sauce* be intoxicating? Reading through the selections was like trying to fathom a foreign dictionary.

"Perhaps you would be kind enough to order my meal, Dr. Holmes? I have to confess, this menu is quite beyond me," and with a rueful smile she handed it over to him.

"Certainly, and please, you can call me Henry. What do you like to eat?"

"My physician advises me to eat seafood whenever possible," she replied, and he didn't press her about this unusual bit of information, but filed it away in the back of his mind.

"Two Lobster Newberg," he told the waiter, "and bring another fork. This one has a spot." He stared hard for a moment at the back of the flustered waiter, carrying away the offending cutlery, before returning his attention to Georgiana.

"So I understand you enjoyed the Auditorium?"

"It was like Ali Baba opened up his cave to the public," she said. "I cannot imagine a more gorgeous space, or more wonderful music."

And with that encouragement he was off, enlightening her with an eloquent discourse on the marvelous concepts of the architecture. He explained how the function of acoustics dictated the elliptical form, then described Sullivan's other projects in the city, and finally, confessed to his own modest efforts at building design.

Henry spoke in a low, smooth voice that captured his listener's attention completely. When he smiled, she felt the corners of her mouth turn up, mirroring his expression, and when he frowned with the effort of detailing some technical point, her own brow knit with concern. His gestures were sharp and precise, the hands small for a man, and his fingernails, she noticed, were perfectly manicured.

By the time their meal arrived, she was rapt.

Her excitement might have suppressed her appetite, but she had never tried lobster before, and after the first morsel, steaming hot and bathed in a luxurious butter-and-cream sauce, she declared to Henry it was the best food she ever had in her life.

———

As OPENING DAY of the World's Fair drew near, the Siegel Cooper department store felt noticeably busier, livelier, with an almost Christmas-like excitement in the air. On the sidewalks of State Street, groups of tourists huddled together, consulting maps and guidebooks and requiring directions. Visits by regular customers decreased, but were more than made up for by newly arrived aliens. First time visitors to a big city were distinguished by their expressions of awe as they wandered through the store. Distinctive accents and foreign languages could be overheard from the lips of well-dressed newcomers, and on one memorable afternoon, a dozen or so tawny men wearing brightly colored, flowing robes meandered right down the main aisle of the store, laughing and pointing and chattering in some exotic tongue, never noticing the astonished stares that followed them.

"Heathens," murmured Nettie, but Georgiana was intrigued.

"I wonder where they're from?"

"As long as they don't stay past the Fair, who cares?" Nettie replied, and Georgiana was silent but inwardly sighed. To expand one's knowledge of the world: wasn't that, after all, the whole purpose of the Fair?

June 29, 1893

Dear Mother,

I'm sorry you did not want to travel, because you would be astonished if you were here.

Now the only question everyone in Chicago asks one another is, what is more wonderful, the Fair during the day or the Fair at night?

I have been to both, and I must conclude, the Fair in the daytime is magnificent, but the night is just a miracle. How can I describe it, what they are calling this "manmade conquest of the dark?"

Suppose you were the size of a mouse, hiding in a dark corner of Cinderella's ballroom. And every lamp, and lantern, and candle in the kingdom covered the huge floor, and above, chandeliers blazed across every inch of the ceiling. Looking out and up from your little hole, that is how the Fair at night would look to you, enormous and brilliant and beyond your comprehension. When a thousand lamps are perfectly reflected in broad lagoons, and colors dance like gypsies in the spray of lighted fountains, you stroll along the Plaza as if in a trance and you don't even hear the crowds. Everyone is hushed by the magical splendor of it all.

And then, the best of all, you climb into the glass cage of the great Ferris Wheel, and up you go, rising and rising into the dark heavens, until it's your turn to pause at the top, and you can look down and see the whole Fair spread out before you like an immense carpet of light.

I'm sure it was right for me to come, though I know you had your doubts, but to live here and to be able to visit the Fair is truly the experience of a lifetime.

I know we agreed Johnny is too young, but he would be thrilled by all this too, especially by the Transportation Building, which all the men like, and the Electricity Building, where they make all the power for the lights and everything (but you'd go deaf if you stayed in there too long, the generators make so much noise!)

I guessed from your last letter that Uncle Isaac has been dropping some hints about a beau. Really, people do jump to conclusions! I've met lots of nice young men, at the store and at church, but certainly feel no rush to encourage any of them. I suppose Uncle Isaac was referring to Dr. Holmes, a mutual friend of ours, a rather older man who has made it his mission to acquaint me with the finer aspects of the city. I will admit it was very pleasant to visit the Fair with someone so well informed.

The alumni group has a boating trip on Lake Michigan next Sunday afternoon, so close by I can walk there right after church. City living really is wonderful!

Your loving daughter,
Georgiana

AFTER THAT FIRST dinner at the Palmer House, and the nighttime visit to the Fair, their friendship was established, and Henry took to stopping by the store at the end of her shift, sometimes just one day a week, sometimes more.

Once the summer finally took hold and the weather was dependably kind, they would stroll east from the store the few blocks to Lake Michigan, enjoying the gently refreshing breeze and newly generous daylight, observing the changed color of the waves with each visit, from a misty gray merging with low clouds, to a restive blue like Henry's eyes, to the languid aqua of hers.

His appearances were erratic. He could never plan them in advance. His several businesses, he explained, were of an ever-changing nature. Although he was a licensed medical doctor, he preferred the pharmacy business to private practice. He acquired extensive real estate holdings, but also dabbled in inventions, for he was fascinated by technology. When a new opportunity came up, he must respond quickly, sometimes with an out of town trip, sometimes with a burst of work, writing contracts, drawing plans, that kept him busy for days at a time. All part of the price, he admitted, of extraordinary ambition.

Henry was not an especially handsome man, nowhere near as attractive in the masculine way as she was in the feminine. He was of medium height, medium build, with unremarkable brown hair, and apart from those compelling eyes, his features were so ordinary he might blend in to any crowd.

Two characteristics stood out. The first was learned by casual observation. He liked to dress formally, well beyond the normal expectations of business attire. The beautifully tailored coat hung a little longer than it had to be, the silk hat reached a bit taller. He resisted the new fashion of using an umbrella for walking, but stayed with a cane, gold-topped, showily expensive.

One discovered the second characteristic by conversing with him. Henry was a brilliant man. His mind was always relentlessly at work, competing with itself, gaining proficiency in the minutiae of various specialties with ease: medicine, pharmacology, contract law, commercial architecture, real estate, even the dull business of insurance.

He seemed to know something about everything, but when he was with her, the subject that engaged him, most flatteringly, was the life of Georgiana Yoke.

He put all sorts of deeply personal questions to her, drawing her out in conversations unlike any she ever had with a man before.

"How did that feel? What were your emotions at that time? It must have been hard for you. Were you sad for long after your father died?"

He listened closely, leaning toward her, taking in every word. He rarely spoke of his own parents, long dead, or of his hometown, far away. All through that spring and summer, he only wanted to talk about her. These revelations seemed to satisfy a wish in Henry to understand everything about her, like an enthralled archeologist decoding a ciphered tablet.

They found a favorite restaurant, quiet and out of the way, serving clam chowder and oyster stew palatable enough to fulfill the requirements of her diet, where they could sit and talk for a long time. He always requested the same special table, cozy and private, and he always chose the same chair back in the corner.

Henry had often observed that most people seemed to enjoy talking about themselves, and that, with only a little encouragement, would gladly confide in him. With his medical training, he long since deduced Georgiana's secret. Now he decided the time had come to hear the whole story from her.

"Georgiana, tell me, how old were you when your illness began?"

SHE WAS EIGHTEEN. It was the day before her graduation from Edinburgh High School, in the spring of 1888. Mary heard a scream, came running, and found Georgiana in near hysterics, holding up a hand mirror.

"My eyes! Something's wrong with my eyes!"

At first Mary thought she meant she was going blind. Georgiana's lovely blue eyes seemed to be bulging right out of their sockets, oddly staring, swollen with tears rolling out of them.

"I look like a fish! I look like a grasshopper," she cried, and a glance at the starched white dress hanging on the back of her door made her cry even harder.

"You must see a doctor," Mary said, but Georgiana refused to leave the house, so Johnny was sent to go and get him.

The doctor's unhappy expression, on first examining her protruding eyes, was not encouraging. He looked at her throat, inside and out, and gently poked her neck and behind her ears. He felt the glands, and led her to the window so he could see her eyes in the bright daylight, pulling the lids up and around.

"Does that hurt?" he asked.

"It feels like pressure, like something is pushing on them from behind."

"Headache?"

"A little."

"Fainting spells lately?"

"Sort of," she said, and Mary started in surprise. Georgiana never said anything about feeling unwell.

"When did this start?"

"Right after Easter."

"What happens when you feel faint?"

"My heart pounds, that's all. It happened in school, and I didn't want to miss," she said, explaining to Mary, and the doctor said, "Go on."

"It only lasts about a minute or two. My heart starts pounding hard, as if I was running fast for a long time, and I come all out in a sweat. I get dizzy. I feel kind of sick at my stomach. My knees get weak and my hands get shaky. It's hard to breathe. Then it's over, and I'm fine again."

"How often does this happen?"

Georgiana shocked her mother again by replying, "Oh, two or three times a day."

"Perhaps we should speak privately, Mrs. Yoke," the doctor said, but Georgiana folded her arms and gave him one of her deepest frowns. He was obviously unused to a household where the opinions of the daughter carried as much weight as those of the parent.

Mary said, "No, that's all right, she can hear it, whatever it is."

"Well," he said, clearing his throat, "it's very likely a symptom of goiter."

Mother and daughter both gasped. Once they had seen a man with a goiter lump the size of an orange on his neck, walking along Main Cross Street. The doctor tried to reassure them.

"I don't feel any growth yet, and it may not happen, but we sometimes see this condition in the eyes come with a goiter. The symptoms you describe all fit. In the worst cases, there is an operation . . ." but he broke off when he saw Mary's face. Like many of the Civil War generation, she felt a special terror of any kind of surgery.

"No reason to think it will come to that," he said. "There's been some very good work done in this area, we may be able to keep it from getting worse."

"What about my eyes?" Georgiana was starting to panic. "What about tomorrow? It's graduation! What will I do?"

"I can't cure you by tomorrow, I'm afraid. You'll have to get through it as best you can. The treatment will take time. We have to send away for something to put in your food."

"My food! Whatever for?"

"Goiter never happens to people who live by the ocean. Only those who live inland, like here in Indiana, ever get it. It's been shown that our diet lacks iodine, and if the patient simply eats products of the sea, which contain iodine, the disease very often reverses itself. At the very least, the symptoms usually get better. That is what you must do," and he pulled out a pad and pencil from his bag, and started writing.

"Oysters, tinned or fresh. Clams, or any ocean fish you can obtain. Kelp, or dried seaweed, I can order for you. You grind it up, and put it in every dish. I'll send it over as soon as the order comes in, I'll get enough for you to use it three times a day, and then I need to see you in two months."

"I'm leaving this summer for college!" she protested, but he ignored that, and turned back to Mary.

"There are a few other things you need to know," he said. "Some people with this condition can become very, well, you might call them sensitive. Moody, you might say. Getting emotionally upset can make it worse."

"That's not me," Georgiana assured the doctor, "my mental state is perfectly fine."

"Bright light could bring on a headache. You may get particularly bothered by heat and by cold," the doctor continued. "In midwinter or midsummer, you may be limited in what you can do."

"Just until the iodine makes me better," she said, and he chose not to explain just then that an ophthalmic goiter was a condition she would deal with for all of her life.

HENRY SET DOWN his fork and leaned back in the booth, satisfied.

"He was a good man. Excellent diagnosis. I'm very impressed that a small town doctor would be up on the latest treatment," and Georgiana felt a little surge of booster pride for Edinburgh. Henry was, after all, a city doctor with his own pharmacy, her new authority on all things medical.

"Do you still feel these symptoms?"

"Sometimes standing at work a long time, I get shaky, but I can hide it, and nobody there knows except my friend Mary Ellen."

"Are you well enough for all that walking in the heat at the Fair?"

"Oh yes, of course. The Fair is why I moved here, after all!"

"I hope the music program next week pleases you as much as the orchestra did."

"They'll have to be very fine to be better than that concert. I can only recall one other time in my life when music affected me so much," and as always, it was this type of remark that captured his interest.

"It was at a Methodist gathering, in Indiana. I was twelve or thirteen. There was a man, a gypsy, or anyway, he was dressed like one. I don't know if that was for real, but he played the violin, all alone, and the notes were so sad and beautiful, they made me cry. I'll never forget it."

Henry studied her, fascinated. The notion of music causing anyone to cry, or of crying itself, was foreign to him.

"Didn't you go to those, growing up?" she asked him. "Any traveling shows, or revivals?"

"I was never much of one for the hallelujah tents," he said.

"Oh, come now, you know it wasn't all preaching. We had opera singers, bands, all kinds of entertainment. One time I remember there was a juggler for the little kids. Some of the inspirational speakers were wonderful, talking about reaching up high for your dreams . . . and after we'd have a big pitch-in supper."

She stopped.

"Oh, I see, you're one of those who make fun, but for those of us out in the country, it was the biggest event of the year."

"A little of that goes a long way," he replied, and this remark concerned her. She could never be serious about a man who lacked religious conviction.

By their next beachfront walk, she had made up her mind to ask him about his religious beliefs directly, and he shocked her with his calm reply.

"I am a follower of Thomas Paine and Robert Ingersoll. I believe, first and foremost, in my personal freedom. You've heard of Robert Ingersoll?"

"I certainly have, I'm sorry to say. He came to a debate in Columbus. Our minister railed against him for half an hour. I'm amazed you put stock in such a blatant atheist."

"Agnostic," Henry corrected her. "He knows Scripture as well, or better, than any of your favorite speakers, like that trumpet-tongue, Mr. Jennings Bryan. You might like some of his positions, if you read them. He opposes corporal punishment of children, isn't that what you said your college professors always went on about?"

"A fool's bolt may sometimes hit the mark," Georgiana quoted.

"He favors suffrage for women, so he's in your camp there."

"We'll have the vote without *his* help," she said, and Henry shook his head at this.

"I'm sorry to tell you, Georgiana, there are two reasons women will never get the vote."

"Oh really, and what might those be?"

"First, you want to use it to impose temperance, and no matter how good your intentions, you can't put a man in jail for drinking."

Georgiana loved this argument. She'd repeated it a hundred times before.

"If a man is willing to risk jail for a drink, that's just proof of the depth of his addiction. All we want is to close the saloons, so they can get free of the habit. I've seen it happen. Once they see what their lives can be, they come over to our side."

Henry shook his head again.

"I've no personal use for alcohol, but I won't let anyone tell me whether or not I may have it."

"So," she said, warming up, "let me see if I understand you. Your atheist, excuse me, agnostic, may go around saying whatever terrible things he wants, but my temperance ladies should be suppressed. Is that it?"

Henry laughed at this deliberate hyperbole.

"I don't say they should be suppressed. On the contrary, I'm for freedom, everyone should say whatever they want to say. I don't care, myself, if women vote or not. I'll grant you this, those who make the argument they are incapable, well, anyone with a mother knows that's false."

"It's just not fair. My mother owns property, pays taxes, so why shouldn't she vote?"

Now she was in her element, agitated and righteous.

"Did I tell you my uncle Nelson served in the Indiana 70th under President Harrison? Can you imagine how exciting it was for him to cast that vote for president, a man who was actually seen by someone in our family? Mother would have been thrilled, to be able to vote for him!"

Henry took her arm in his, and patted her hand.

"So what is the second reason?" she said. "You said there were two reasons women won't get the vote."

"Yes, I did. Very well, here's the second. Men sell their votes. It's a business, and it works very well for their purposes. Women voting would ruin it. That's all." He allowed a moment for her to absorb this unpleasant truth.

Georgiana was shocked, not only by his words, but his bluntness in sharing them.

"Don't think it's limited to the big cities, like Chicago. The same game is played everywhere, your little Danville, or Edinburgh, whatever town you care to name. Big towns and small, the vote is a cheat and a fraud."

"But if a ballot is secret, how is that done?" she argued. "They might pay a man to cast a vote, but how could they know how he actually voted?"

"Oh, there are many ways," he answered, and his nonchalance annoyed her. She pressed for an example, so he obliged.

"The voter being paid is called a floater. The floater puts a secret mark on the ballot, the election clerk is bribed to watch for it, and if it is voted the way they want, then the floater is paid off."

She didn't say anything, but folded her hands and studied the churning, muck-colored waves.

"Georgiana, here's the truth. Corruption is all around us, in places you would never expect. Elections are corrupt, judges are corrupt, police and prosecutors and building inspectors – all of them are rotten! Don't ever forget that. To succeed in your aspiration to vote will take a miracle, because you're up against a system that only wants power for itself."

She stayed silent, weighing his words so long he finally looked down at her, to determine if she was upset by his bitter tone, but she did not seem to be. Eventually, she smiled at him, back to her usual assured, serene self.

"You're wrong, Henry," she said. "I believe, in our lifetimes, there will be suffrage for women, and, because of it, just as you say, temperance laws will be passed. And the world will be a better place for it."

GEORGIANA'S CRUSADING IDEALISM dated back to her college days.

Few places have ever enjoyed a more cordial town-and-gown relationship than Danville, Indiana, and the Central Normal College, which located there in 1878. Part of the local pride in the school was due to its dramatic arrival to the community, which happened overnight. A Professor Harper made the flattering decision to move his school of forty-eight students from their outgrown facilities in Ladoga, Indiana, to Danville, leading a caravan of wagons filled with the supplies of the school, the male students and their possessions. The female students took the train through Greencastle, and classes commenced the next day, a feat that became legendary in Danville.

The school brought a wonderful financial advantage to the town. The college never built dormitories, but instead made arrangements so all the students might board in the homes of the townspeople. This not only provided a reliable stream of extra income, but also created deep personal connections between the citizens and the students.

By the time Georgiana arrived there, in 1888, the school enrolled nearly five hundred students, and Danville was a fairly small town, with a population of about fifteen hundred persons. So virtually every household was in the landlord business, charging about $2.00 a week for a shared room and board with a private family, making the students a beloved part of the local economy.

There was a strong spiritual affinity between the college and the dry town. The school catalog boasted that, in addition to its healthful and beautiful location, intelligent and industrious residents, and six vigorous churches, there was not one single drinking saloon to be found within ten miles of Danville in any direction.

A vast network teacher's colleges like this one, called Normal schools, developed after the Civil War. Followers of the "Normal Idea" were called "Normalites." They espoused revolutionary principles such as: Study can be made more attractive than mischief;

Individuality of the pupil is sacred; Co-education of the sexes is essential to intellectual development, good behavior and purity; A true teacher is always a friend and guide, never a boss or master.

Into this heady environment poured a fresh wave of optimistic young people, the post-Civil War generation already taking for granted new marvels like telephones and electric lights. The school was a wonderful fit for Georgiana's strong personality, molding her from a smart and energetic girl to a young woman of firm principles and lofty ideals.

She cut a wide swath back in Danville, and later in Columbus. Plenty of young men hoped to squire her around to restaurants and the theatre, but none of them quite lived up to her expectations. She learned to carefully sift through revealing statements of potential beaus, running them through her moral sieve. And after four months of keeping company with Henry, eligible as he was and pleasant as many occasions were, she had to admit he fell short of her requirements.

To begin with, she just assumed he was a member at the Methodist Corner. But no, he claimed he simply enjoyed hearing a well thought out sermon from time to time, and so he occasionally dropped in at a variety of churches. This want of commitment made absolutely no sense to her.

Then, his lack of political awareness was infuriating, as well as a complete waste of a vote. His advocacy of social liberties was alarming, and all her very best arguments made no impact.

"So, if I understand you correctly, elections are swayed by bribing immigrants, yet you have no stand on the immigration question?" she challenged him, riled by Methodist nationalism, but he merely shrugged his shoulders, not worried in the least about the influence of the Irish or the Germans.

"My only stand," he repeated, "is freedom to pursue my business as I choose," and that confirmed his final disqualification. Henry was devoted to work, constantly, feverishly, to a degree that even she, who admired ambition, found unsettling.

He appeared at the store at the end of her shift after an absence of a week, haggard, shadows like bruises ringing his eyes. He was engaged in a prolonged negotiation to launch a complicated but lucrative project, he explained, building a factory to manufacture a duplicating machine of his own invention, in which an original document was wrapped around a cylinder coated with ink. By simply turning a crank, any number of exact copies of the document could be produced in a matter of minutes. He was so engrossed in perfecting the design of his machine that he forgot to sleep.

"Did you never hear that money is the root of all evil?" she asked, only partly teasing.

"*Radix malorus est cupiditas*," he replied. "You need to review Timothy, it's the *desire* for mammon alone that ensnares people. I'm in no danger, because I regard it simply for what it is, a tool, a means to an end."

"But what is the end, if your mind is always on work?"

"I have other plans, and they extend far beyond Chicago."

He halted their walk, taking a moment to stare out over the water and compose his speech.

"It's hard for those of us, people like you, and me, who grew up pinching our pennies, to learn to think of money in any other terms than necessity. We were not reared among the upper classes. I look at men around us, great successful men, and I wonder, are they happy? Marshall Field works as many hours as I do, is he happy? Who knows? If my only goal was to sell more finery than anyone else, I guess his life would be enough for me.

"But that is not my ambition. My new copy machine will change the way business is done, relieve untold hours of tedious labor, it will make a real difference in the world, in progress! That's where my satisfaction lies. And with it, if it brings me great wealth, and I believe it will, then comes freedom. That's the true value of money, freedom to do what one wishes. And if one has a larger vision, a wish, a desire to exercise that freedom to change the world for the better, then money becomes the means, not the end.

"And I have a larger vision, Georgiana. I'm a self-made man, and I foresee for myself a life of purpose, of influence. A life of, yes, prosperity, with some of the good things money can buy, for who should not enjoy what he has earned? Do you see any of our city fathers apologizing for their extravagances? No, indeed! And yet, who builds the orphanages and hospitals? Who plans the bridges, the water works, the schools and colleges? Who put together the Fair itself? Do you not see, Georgiana, how limited is your argument that a bit of overwork, in the pursuit of a dream, must be a bad thing?" He paused at last, cheeks flushed, eyes bright.

She was amazed. He never talked about himself like this before.

"Put like that, I guess I do see your point. When guided by responsibility, and sober self-control, much good can be done. But wealth should be gotten on Christian principles."

"Ha!" Henry said. "Do you think the railroads were built on Christian principles? Were the banks? No, unfortunately, the world of business is a hard, ruthless place."

"I work in a business. I don't think it's the way you describe."

"Your bosses do. They deal with all the rough-and-tumble. You simply charm the customers into buying their merchandise. You're sheltered from what happens behind their doors."

"Nevertheless," she said, coming back to the point, "we all choose the way we conduct our lives."

"Indeed, we certainly do. You and I both chose our own path. I do wonder, why you, for example, gave up teaching altogether and moved here, rather than just come for the summer, visit the Fair, and return home. That's what most teachers would have done."

Georgiana flushed a little, uncertain of how the subject had changed to her. "The truth is," and this was difficult, for she hated to confess to such a weakness in herself, "the truth is, I was not a very good schoolteacher. I got on well enough, but when faced with spending the whole day at school, every day, perhaps for the rest of my life, the simple truth of it is, I was bored."

There, she had said it, out loud. Guilt over wasting her education gnawed at her conscience for months, and now the painful admission was out in the open. She glanced over, to see if he looked disgusted with her, and was relieved. He smiled with complete understanding.

"I tried to be interested in the students, I really did, but my mind would wander. I felt like the classroom was as confining for me as it was for them! Then, there was my medical condition. If my eyes swelled up, and I got the shakes, the children would notice, and the little ones would say things. That was very hard for me. When the Fair was announced, it was all I could think of. I never intended to come for just a visit. I knew I needed something else besides teaching. But everyone fought me on it, and I could never tell the real reason. I'm just not very good, or patient, with children."

"You are far too hard on yourself."

She listened to his voice, soft and comforting.

"If you have your own, you'll feel differently. I'm sure you were just as kind and good as any of the other teachers. What's not your fault, of course, is your mind is too active, too broad, your ambitions lay beyond the classroom of a small town school."

She didn't know what to say to this, and they walked on for a while, until he stopped, and gestured towards a park bench. They sat, and his arm reached across her back, and then for the first time he rested his hand, warm and secure, on her shoulder. She didn't object.

"I'm struck by how very similar we are, Georgiana. Like you, I was bored with my first medical practice. To study, to learn the wonders of the human form, was my greatest joy. Then to find myself doomed to sit in an office and listen to complaints of gout all day? No, I could not do it. And, consider this. We've both suffered loss, at a very young age, and had to work hard and struggle for our success. Both of us grew discontented with the ordinary, with an existence that would have satisfied many, perhaps, but was not enough for us. We both took a risk, coming here to the city, on our own, with nothing but our wits and our drive."

In reality, she knew this wasn't exactly true. She had a family to fall back on, and her uncle's kindness in a place to live. But she buried that thought, and allowed in its place the more compelling image of a brave and heroic quest.

Henry summed up.

"We both want more than the gritty life of business. We want to live in a world that is fine, among people with larger ideas, grander schemes for the future, a world of ideals, of progress. You wish to cure the world of its addictions. I want to purge it of its sickness."

"Henry," she said, moved and overwhelmed.

He squeezed her shoulder.

"You're such a good influence on me, Georgiana. I want to see you, be with you, much more often in the future."

"I would like that too," she said. Then she added, "And I'm looking forward to meeting your circle of friends."

That stumped him. He thought quickly, eyes scanning the vast lake, back and forth, as though reading a line of text far out on the horizon.

She immediately berated herself for her presumption, but very soon, she was reassured.

"They will all be envious," he said, "when they see me with you."

If Georgiana had any notion that this most intimate conversation would lead straight to a proposal, she was soon set right. Henry walked her to her uncle's door, gave her a chaste shake of the hand, and vanished. She waited, but for nearly three weeks she didn't get a message, or a letter, or a telegram from him.

By the time he finally reemerged, she had reluctantly convinced herself that he must have changed his mind about her. Perhaps he met someone else? But now he appeared at the store, anxious and hurried, asking her to dine with him after work. She was tempted to say she needed advance notice to make an engagement, but he was so insistent, had something so important to tell her, that she relented.

Seated in their favorite restaurant, secluded in their special corner, he took a deep, preparing breath.

"I apologize for not sending you a note, explaining my absence, but this has been a rather eventful time for me. I had to go away. Several things happened, significant things, and my life has taken an altogether unexpected turn."

"I did wonder what happened to you," she admitted.

"First, a lawyer wrote to me, to tell me my uncle died, and left me a deed to his property in Texas. You can only imagine my surprise."

She made an expression of condolence, but he held up his hand.

"I didn't know him personally. He was my father's younger brother, long estranged from the family. Remind me some day to tell you the details of that quarrel! It was a terrible breach, never healed. So sad."

His eyes blinked a few times as he buttered his bread. She was touched by this, and by now in complete suspense.

"Soon after this, I completed that business contract I've been working on, the lease of land for a factory in Germany. An investor wants to manufacture my machine if I can raise a certain amount of venture capital in a year. This has long been my ambition, but I couldn't find a suitable partner until now, someone with the technical expertise and experience I need. This inheritance, in Fort Worth, will give me the financial safety to really make this business work. So, the long and short of it is, I'm leaving Chicago, perhaps forever."

He stopped, watching closely for any sign of dismay. She struggled to keep her expression neutral, concealing a sudden lurching in her stomach of surprising intensity. Just an hour ago, she had no idea where she stood in his regard. Now, at the prospect of truly never seeing him again, she felt cheated, like a good child on Christmas morning beholding a lump of coal.

"I've decided to sell my pharmacy, and close up my other businesses. Mr. Quinlan, my caretaker, will handle rents from my tenants next year, after which time I'll decide if it makes more sense to continue as a landlord, or sell the building. I'll leave for Texas at the start of the New Year, as soon as the legal matters of the will are completed. After that, I'll travel for several months, gathering investors for the project. By next fall, I expect to be on a ship to Germany. I'll be there for at least a year, maybe two."

This must surely mean goodbye. She could hardly expect an engagement to last three years and across an ocean. She waited.

"I want you with me," he said quietly. "I want to marry you before I go to Texas. I do not want to make this journey alone."

Her stomach lurched a second time. Before she could respond, or even gather her thoughts, he stopped her, holding up his finger to his lips.

"Don't speak yet, Georgiana. In fact, I don't want you to make up your mind until tomorrow. I must tell you some things first, before you give me your answer. I want to be utterly truthful with you, to be frank in all matters. Is that all right?"

"Of course, if that's really what you want, Henry," she answered. "I do need to hear all you have to say."

He hesitated, evidently pained by what he must now disclose.

"I am not a young man, at least, not as young and green as I was when I came to this city. There have been, in my life, two women, of importance. It would be dishonest if I did not disclose this to you.

"When I was very young, just a boy, really, I lost my parents. Perhaps I was lonely, perhaps I just wanted to attach myself to another family, I don't know, I'll never know, really, why I did it. But I was very enamored with a local girl, we went to school together, and after high school I persuaded her to elope with me."

He took a sip of water, and then he stared intently into the glass, as if images from his past were floating there.

"In less than a week, we both knew it was a terrible mistake. We returned to her parent's home, and confessed our true feelings. Well, her family, bless them, was very forgiving, amazingly so, really, and took her back. Her father knew someone, a high up person in court, who found some technicality in the law, and had the marriage annulled. It was at that time I decided to leave New Hampshire, go to medical school, and make my own way in the world."

"What happened to the girl?" Georgiana didn't want to interrupt his narrative, but curiosity got the better of her.

"What happened to her? Oh, well, I heard she married someone else. I sent an announcement upon graduation from medical school to some folks back there, folks interested in my welfare, and that year I actually received a Christmas greeting and congratulations from her family! Can you imagine such kindness? I was truly touched by that," and he sighed a little, and she could see it all, the bereaved young man, romantic and impulsive, so in love with his childhood sweetheart he couldn't wait to marry her.

"But I think she has since died," he added.

"Died! How?"

"I ran into a schoolmate, last year. He said he heard one of the girls in our class died in childbirth, and from his description, I think it might have been she. I didn't have the heart to write her family and inquire."

They sat without speaking for a little while, until she gently brought him back to the present.

"What happened next?"

"Ah, well, the next," and now the tone turned from sorrowful to bitter.

"I came to Chicago, after several false starts, that medical practice I told you about, some other ventures, until I found the pharmacy business most to my liking. I bought a store, and gained some success. But before I purchased the Englewood property, and began my building, I met a woman."

Georgiana had a definite feeling she was not going to like this chapter as well as the first one, and she was right.

"She seemed respectable, at first. I was, as I say, young and green and unused to the ways of the city, and lonely." He gave her a curious look. "Much of my life has been lonely, either from too much work, as you have pointed out, or perhaps, you may laugh at this, a bit of shyness. At any rate, I was flattered by her attention to me. She is a bit older than I am, and, as I found out, was more experienced in life as well.

"Too late, I found out what she really was — an opportunistic adventuress, just after me for her own gain. She came to me, one day, and confessed she was expecting a child, but did not want to marry me. She only wanted financial support."

Georgiana looked down at her plate.

"Being a doctor, I know something of these things. There was only the slightest possibility that the baby was mine, yet I felt, since I had committed the sin, that I should pay the penalty. I knew full well, by that time, there were other men in her life, both before me and since, but I went ahead and set her up in a house. She has a daughter, now four years old. She lives in Wilmette, way out north of here, known to the neighbors as a widow. I simply don't believe that a child should be held responsible for the sins of the parents," and now he met her eyes, as if challenging her to condemn his actions.

"But the child," Georgiana said, "is she all right? I mean, living with such a person, is she a fit mother to rear a child? Might she not be neglectful?"

"Oh, well, once born, the child became her be-all and end-all. If anything, she is spoiled too much! Heaven knows, she is constantly asking for more money, for outfits and walking buggies and toys, then there will be private schooling — no, neglect is not the problem. The real worry is that she's never going to let go of her grip on me. Though she refused marriage, she still wished to claim my exclusive attention, and when I made it clear I wanted to assert my freedom, she only became more possessive, not less so. It's a form of madness that happens to some women. When they are denied the thing they want, it makes the desire only stronger. I cannot tell you more than that, for we had an ugly quarrel that would only distress you to know of. She would, it goes without saying, be beside herself with jealousy if she knew anything of you."

Of course, Georgiana realized, this must be why he never introduced her to his friends. Word might get back to this monstrous woman, this menace, who would cause scenes, increase her demands, make threats of who knew what terrible things. What a dreadful situation. No wonder he seemed sad sometimes, lost in his own thoughts, dwelling on his past mistakes. Of course his sin had been bad, his judgment even worse, but he had tried to atone, done what he could, and would pay for it many times over. No, her sympathy was largely with him.

"I had to go out there, a few days ago, to make arrangements for next year. She carried on dreadfully, even got Lucy upset and crying — Lucy, that's the little girl's name — until I promised to send a doll from Germany. And so I will. I do keep my promises."

He walked her home through the warm summer evening, through streets lively with diners, strollers, Fair-goers and late-night workers. Georgiana never felt so much a part of Chicago as now, when she was being invited to leave it. At the apartment door, he pulled a small jeweler's box from his pocket.

"Don't open it tonight," he said. "Think everything over, very carefully. You're still so young, you must not make a hasty decision.

I'm asking a lot, I know, to be away from your friends, your family, for such a long time. I don't want you to say yes unless you're very sure," and she thought she detected, for the second time that night, tears in his eyes as he placed a gentle kiss on her forehead and turned away.

"I'll call for you here at seven o'clock tomorrow. Sleep well."

She went inside, closed the door and made herself wait a full ten minutes before opening the box.

GEORGIANA SAT BY herself, small in the vaulted space of the church.

That morning she sent a messenger boy to deliver a note to her supervisor, saying she was too sick to work today. She had never done such a thing before, but, she told herself, it was a little true. A restless night will make anyone feel ill. Add to it a low, steady excitement, a possibility of imminent change, and an ordinary workday becomes an impossible burden.

She could not concern herself with handkerchiefs today, she could only think of Henry's offer. He wasn't just another boy to flirt with, and then retreat if it was not to her liking. This was a man, a serious, older, professional man, and now was the time to make up her mind if he was the one she really wanted. Was this tumultuous feeling an infatuation, or was this love?

A whole morning in bed had not helped her make up her mind, nor had a walk to the lake, through the park, along the street, carefully skirting the Siegel Cooper block. Only prayer, she realized, would help, but even after an hour in this pew, the velvet box remained shut in her purse.

She couldn't deny she was attracted to him. A life by his side would never be dull. And who else ever took the trouble to understand her so completely? What other man would appreciate her intelligence, or invite her confidences, or debate important issues with her?

And as a provider, well, he had no competition there. Was she supposed to disregard that? Should she silence that practical voice in her head, pointing out the obvious, *you need never think of hand-kerchiefs, ever again! Johnny's education, Mary's old age, both secure with a simple "I will!"*

But those revelations over dinner must give her serious pause. He openly admitted to a feckless past, an eccentric pattern of living, and an irreligious focus on worldly success. Could she find a way to overlook those faults?

After a long while, she took the Book from the shelf before her, and held it on her lap, slowly fanning the pages. She closed her eyes and let her index finger land randomly on a page.

My brethren, if any one among you wanders from the truth and some one brings him back, let him know that whoever brings back a sinner from the error of his way will save his soul from death and will cover a multitude of sins.

Georgiana studied this passage for a long while, slowly reread all of James, and then closed the Book with relief.

Now everything was clear. Now everything was justified. Now it was possible to say yes without reservation. How selfish she had been, to consider the proposal from her own desires, her own advantage. *Henry* was the one who needed *her*. From this day forward, she would be his guide.

She paid no attention to the growing heat of the day, or to other visitors entering and leaving the church. When the afternoon sun reached the gloriously colored windows, its rays illuminating the eternal story they told, she opened her purse and took out the jeweler's box.

———

IN CHICAGO, IN the late summer, every now and again, a gift arrives from Canada. A powerful mass of fresh air skims the surface of the chilly lake, absorbing its refreshing cold. It blasts through streets and alleys, driving humidity, coal smoke, and the stench of the stockyards far out onto the western plains.

The atmosphere left behind is sweet, brisk, invigorating. Trees and buildings look sharp as etchings against the blue sky. Residents who complained the day before about the stultifying heat now look for reasons to get out of doors. Office boys envy their construction worker brothers. Mothers push buggies to the parks and along the lakefront in pairs and in groups. Shoppers emerge and throng on the sidewalks, lingering between the great department stores on State Street.

On one such day, at the Siegel Cooper department store, Harry Chapman was surprised to see Mary Ellen Ladd adjusting her hat in the employee cloakroom mirror at only 10:30 in the morning.

"Are you well, Mrs. Ladd?" he asked, though she looked just fine.

"Oh yes, I'm having a holiday today. I'm owed some time off for working late, so I'm off to the Fair for the afternoon."

"You don't say! What a splendid day for it. Your defection is well timed!"

"It's lucky it just turned out that way. We made this arrangement to get together after Miss Yoke quit the store."

That caught his interest.

"Do you know why she left? Everyone misses her."

"No, I was home sick for a week, and when I came back she was gone. I suspect she found the job too tiring. Maybe she'll tell me about it today. I'm meeting her for lunch in an hour."

"Are you really," he said.

"I've been looking forward to a visit. The lunchroom is pretty dull without her company, and as you say, you couldn't ask for a nicer day. The Fair is not so pleasant when it's hot, with all the crowds, but today should be perfect."

"I've been thinking of going myself," Harry said. "I've been over there at night, but never during an afternoon. It's really almost a duty, in a way, to support them," he added, noting the pamphlet in Mary Ellen's hand. The management of Siegel Cooper published a special guidebook for its employees. Everyone was expected to patronize the Fair at least once in the season, to help ensure its success.

"You needn't persuade me, I'd give you the day off if I could!" Mary Ellen laughed, and Harry looked thoughtful.

"Actually, I'm owed some extra time as well, and I know they'd rather pay in time than money! Would you like an escort on the train, if I can arrange it?"

Mary Ellen hesitated. Georgiana specifically said in her note she had something particular to discuss. Perhaps she wouldn't want the added company, and they had so few chances to get together these days.

On the other hand, an arm to lean on through the crowded city was always welcome, and Harry need not stay with them through the whole visit. She nodded, and Harry rushed off to prevail upon his boss and assign tasks to the porters in his absence. In less than ten minutes it was done, and just like that, instead of a routine shift of forgettable labor, they were off to the World's Fair on the finest day of the summer.

It took just twelve minutes by train to get from downtown to the fairgrounds on the south side of the city. Once there, Harry graciously paid Mary Ellen's admission, over her protests, but after all, he argued, it was thanks to her that he was there at all. Otherwise he'd still be at work, gazing out of windows and longing to enjoy the outdoors.

Mary Ellen felt relieved that Georgiana expressed no reservations over the addition of Harry. She acted delighted to see him, and seemed perfectly well, in fact even more animated than usual. The three strolled, happily, among the crowds, giggling and even laughing out loud at Harry's ridiculous banter; where in the world did *that* tourist come from, which member of the Lady's Committee chose *that* exhibit, should he apply at the Midway for a job doing the infamous hootchie-koochtie dance?

They laughed when they discovered all three of them were wearing new hats, courtesy of the bankrupt sale shelf at Siegel Cooper. They kept on laughing, because they were free for the whole afternoon, and had the pleasure of knowing at this moment how it felt to be young on a beautiful summer day at the greatest Fair in the most exciting city in the world.

The ladies turned the brims of their new hats against the dazzling white of the buildings. Many in the crowd carried small umbrellas and some men wore dark glasses.

Like everyone else, the three friends wandered and pointed and exclaimed and were enthralled.

They shopped for souvenirs. Georgiana selected a Chinese fan for Mary, useful for church in hot weather, but hesitated over a display of treats for her brother Johnny. Harry pointed over her shoulder to bright packs of Juicy Fruit chewing gum, inexpensive and easy to ship. She picked up a package and studied it.

"Better send enough for the fellows on his team," Harry advised, "didn't you say your brother is a baseball man? What he really wants, you know, is to be the hero and treat his pals," and she smiled in gratitude. She really had no idea what a boy would want. Just to confirm the rightness of the choice, Harry bought a supply as a gift for the porters, and they carried on in search of refreshments.

Later, sipping cool lemonades in the shade of the pavilion, Georgiana could no longer contain herself, and confided to her friends the startling news of her engagement. They had both seen Henry at the store once or twice, but neither of them had any idea of a serious courtship. Mary Ellen looked a little shocked, and Harry's good humor vanished.

"What, you mean that old fellow?"

Harry blurted out this thoughtless response, and felt the tip of Mary Ellen's boot on his shin.

Georgiana didn't seem to mind their lack of enthusiasm. She merely smiled, and said, "He's only a little over thirty."

Harry quickly backtracked.

"That is, congratulations Miss Yoke! Everyone at the store, I'm sure, will be delighted for you, though some girls on the selling floor will be jealous of your conquest!"

Mary Ellen added her congratulations, but then asked, "Isn't this very fast, Georgiana? Has your mother even met him yet?"

"No, not yet, but we'll go to Franklin this fall. As to haste, well, Henry must travel all next year on business, around the country and then on to Germany, maybe for another year after that, and he wants me with him. There didn't seem to be any good reason to wait, once our minds were made up," and she removed her thin lace glove to reveal a very fine ring, silver and studded with small diamonds and sapphires, and that made it final. Her companions stared in silence for a moment, until Harry pushed back his chair, forcing his usual broad smile.

"Well, I can see where this conversation is heading! All lace veils, and trousseaus, and travel rags, and everything a man knows nothing about. So I'll let you get to it."

He turned to Mary Ellen.

"Mrs. Ladd, thanks for letting me join you. This was the most enjoyable day I've had in a long time. I'll see you next week at the store. Miss Yoke," he said, reaching across the table to shake her hand. "I sincerely do wish you all the best. That doctor is a lucky man. Maybe you'll send a postcard to the store from your travels," and she patted his hand and assured him it would be done, and thanked him for his help.

"Well, this is good-bye, then."

The two women sipped their drinks and watched Harry walk away, slowly twirling his hat on his finger and whistling an odd little tune.

2

INDIANA

Fall 1893 – January 1894

It had been Henry's wish, once their engagement was official, that Georgiana quit her job at Siegel Cooper. Although he could not yet in decency take over the entire responsibility of supporting her, he worried those long hours of standing were bad for her health. He was so concerned that her condition might recur he spent an hour in the back room of his pharmacy, making up a special relaxing tonic just for her.

She wanted to remain in the city for the fall, as there was so much more of the Fair to experience, and Henry found the perfect solution, a part-time job at the Fair itself, easy work in the cloakroom.

They worked out a plan. She would stay with Uncle Isaac until the week of her twenty-fourth birthday, in October, and then she and Henry would take the train together to her mother's home in Franklin to meet the family. He would return to the city to conclude his business affairs, leaving her in Franklin until Christmas. Then they would marry and begin their travels.

Oddly, their time together, now they were actually engaged, was even more irregular and sporadic than before. Sometimes a note would arrive by a messenger, at the apartment or the cloak-room at the Fair, letting her know he would pick her up at a certain time, or she should meet him at their restaurant that evening.

One day after her shift at the Fair cloakroom, they took a quick train ride to Englewood for a tour of his property. She remembered what the girl in the Jewelry department told her, that his World's Fair hotel covered a whole city block. It was indeed a vast building, more extensive and imposing than she ever expected, four stories high, with high, red-brick walls and turrets, striking curved stained glass windows, frescoed stucco walls, black and white diamond floor tiling, all of his own design, tasteful and impressive. On the street level they visited the phar-macy, the jewelry shop, and a quick peek at his private office, but he could not show her any of the upper level hotel rooms, since all of them were occupied.

There was a steady clacking from behind a door near his office, and when he opened it she saw two rows of desks occupied by about a dozen typewriter girls, all pecking away with intimidating efficiency. She had tried typing once herself and found it an impos-sible skill to learn. She nodded and smiled around the room at the employees of her fiancé, and her eyes locked, for just an instant, with those of a brown haired, round faced girl, and the unmistak-able bitterness in her look sent a shock through Georgiana.

"Henry," she said later, "one of those girls seemed upset by my visit," and he laughed.

"Jealous of you, of course. One of the many advantages of mov-ing away will be freedom from the theatrics of secretaries!"

Unlike Harry and Mary Ellen, Mary Yoke was delighted with the news of Georgiana's engagement. As the promised October visit to her small home in Franklin, Indiana drew near, she busied herself with happy plans and quandaries: what to serve, what to wear, where to put an overnight guest. When Georgiana was in

Franklin she had to share a bedroom with Mary. Should they borrow a cot and have Henry sleep in the other bedroom with Johnny?

No, of course not, Georgiana assured her, Henry would stay at the hotel. He would need privacy to work during his stay. Mary shouldn't worry about putting him up.

Uncle Nelson, disappointingly, was not nearly so celebratory.

"I congratulate you, of course," he wrote, *"and everyone wishes you great happiness. I regret, however, that I did not have a chance to meet your intended before you accepted him. I made a promise to your father to look after you, now I feel I failed in that office.*

"Marry in haste, repent at leisure, they say, and I think you should reconsider the timing of this. You'll have a lifetime to spend with each other. A mature love can postpone immediate wants. Please make sure you know your own heart, and do not let the lure of travel or financial security influence your choice — Society can be very unforgiving if that motive is suspected."

Georgiana was livid.

"Society," she wrote back, *"can't quite decide what it wants. If a girl merely steps out with numerous beaus, and no commitment follows, she is called frivolous, and her reputation is in danger. If she grows serious with a young man, whose career prospects are yet unknown, then she is called reckless. If she becomes engaged to an older, successful man, she is considered mercenary. This is a balancing act that could defeat the world's greatest tightrope walker!"*

She heedlessly shoved her answer into the post office slot, even though she knew it would hurt her uncle's feelings. She stayed upset for the rest of the day, and decided, since he had so much else on his mind, to not even mention her uncle's letter to Henry.

The week before their planned trip to Franklin, word came that her grandmother, Isabelle Yoke, had suffered a stroke and was gravely ill. Georgiana felt conflicted about taking Henry with her out to the family farm. It was her duty and desire to make the visit, of course, but it was not at all the time or place to introduce Henry to Nelson and the other uncles. Henry himself expressed a worry about this. He certainly hesitated to intrude on the family during a time of serious illness.

As it turned out, the problem solved itself. Henry was delayed by a business trip, so Georgiana traveled on ahead of him, paying a visit to the farm by herself on the way through Indianapolis.

The farmhouse Richason and Isabelle Yoke built was a comfortable haven, plain white, two stories high and fronted by a deep porch with four sturdy pillars. Tall windows without shutters lit the two spacious rooms that comprised each floor. The large dining room and kitchen were in a wing. The smokehouse was attached to the kitchen, where Isabelle had cooked for fifty years on an open fireplace fitted with cranes. The property also had a poultry house, a carriage house, and two barns.

A cozy sort of beauty prevailed inside. Four-poster beds with feather mattresses filled the upstairs. A floral patterned carpet graced the parlor. Grooved walnut trim, harvested from timber cut for the frame of the house, ran throughout, polished and rubbed so smooth that a child could run her hand along the entire length of it and never catch a splinter.

Uncle George, the youngest of the Yoke brothers, came up the dirt road to greet her. He alone had kept the farm operations going in the two decades since his father died, staying with his mother as the rest of the siblings married and moved away. This was the hardest of all for him, since everyone knew the time would soon come for the 160 acres to be divided between all the heirs of Isabelle and Richason Yoke.

George showed her around a while first, pointing out changes since her last visit: a new calf, an improved road, a tree split from a lightning strike. In the distance she heard the rumbling of a freight train.

"I remember when Father sold the right-of-way," George said. "He hated to do it, of course, but 'we must support the farmers' was his motto, and the train carries the grain. The whole family went out to watch, the first day the train went through, a big black noisy beast puffing its way across our field! After a while everyone else got used to it, though I never really did."

"You wouldn't like Chicago, then, the street noise never stops," Georgiana said. "I forgot how peaceful it is out here."

"It's good for Mother," George said. "She wouldn't ever want to be anywhere else," and as they went inside, Georgiana looked at the staircase and sighed.

"I had better go up. Will she know me?"

"I think so," he lowered his voice, "but she goes in and out. Sit a while, she'll like to see you when she wakes up."

Georgiana slipped up the stairs to her grandmother's bedroom and sat down to wait in a stuffed chair by the open window. The last time she occupied this spot was on a brutally hot day, in 1880, thirteen years ago. She rested in the chair and remembered looking out that same window.

HER FATHER'S FUNERAL was not set to begin until two o'clock, but by noon she counted a dozen wagons and buggies already settled in along the quarter mile of dirt road between the house and Shelby Street. She pitied the horses, slick with sweat and bullied by flies, patiently waiting for someone to lead them to water and shade.

The room felt as if someone had just opened an oven door, so that with every intake of breath, the air singed her nostrils. Above the cornfields, in the distance, a heat mirage shimmered in a mocking imitation of water.

Mourners slowly climbed down from their vehicles, holding up cloth-covered baskets, armloads of flowers, extra chairs. She recognized some of the aunts and uncles and cousins and neighbors, bustling figures all in black except for some veterans in their Union blue military jackets.

Across the hall, she could just make out softened footsteps and low voices and a door closing, as female relatives deposited necessary items in the other bedroom: spare mourning clothes for now, cornstarch and dry corsets for later.

They were careful not to disturb Georgiana and her mother. This was their time to rest, and in fact Mary, unaccustomed to the leisure of a lie-down in the middle of the day, quickly dozed off. Obliging cousins, thankfully, had whisked baby Johnny away to the barn to pet some new kittens. There was nothing for Georgiana to do now but watch out the window and think and wait, until finally it was time to go downstairs.

Johnny had thrown a tantrum when he was taken from the kittens, and now lay fast asleep on Grandmother Isabelle's bed, moist from humidity and spent rage, only occasionally giving out a sobbing hiccup. Lord willing, he would stay that way for the duration of the service.

Georgiana retightened Mary's garments for her. Mary brushed out Georgiana's hair and started a braid.

"No, Mother, braids are for school!"

Mary sighed. This was not a day for vanity or a battle of wills, but she could seldom find the strength to oppose Georgiana.

"It's too hot to wear it down," she said mildly. "And it looks disrespectful to let it hang loose."

"I'll put it up, then." Georgiana held a bunch of hair off her neck, but Mary shook her head.

"Eleven is too young to wear it like that."

She rummaged through a dresser drawer and came up with a length of black velvet ribbon, and in the end Georgiana was satisfied, pulling up the top and sides together, securing the length with a severe knot instead of a bow.

The black made a pleasing contrast against the flax-colored hair. Mary adjusted the dark dress they had cut down for Georgiana, took her arm, and together they went down the stairs.

The first to greet them with a sympathetic hug was Uncle Nelson, the brother next in age to her father. His wife, Isabelle, was by his side. Her first name was really Caroline, and her middle name Isabelle, but the joke of the family was that Nelson liked his own mother so much, only another Isabelle would do, so that's what they called her.

It had been Nelson's task to sit up all last night beside his brother's body, and despite his soldierly bearing, the tiredness showed. His face was pale, and sweat trickled from his high hairline.

Aunt Isabelle took Georgiana's arm gently in her own, and walked with her to the coffin in the parlor for a final goodbye. The closed lid was draped with phlox and primroses, tansy and marigolds, and sprigs of fragrant rosemary, but in this heat, the coffin couldn't remain much longer in the house. It would be loaded in the wagon right after the funeral, and then early tomorrow morning begin the ten-mile journey to Crown Hill Cemetery.

The Methodist minister arrived, and with the other men set about making the shady part of the yard into a holy place. Most of the visitors brought at least one kitchen chair. More were carried out from the house, so at least all the women could sit. Rows like pews were set, and a dictionary stand became a lectern for the minister's notes and his Book, with white lilies arranged below it. One man sat off to the side with a guitar.

The high wall of corn did not rustle at all. The air and the people sat perfectly still. The only movements were the small ones of some women's hands, lightly fanning a face, or gently patting a baby on the back. No one made a sound until the first hymn.

Lo! The prisoner is released,
Lightened of his fleshly load,
Where the weary are at rest,
He is gathered unto God!
Lo! The pain of life is past,
All his warfare now is o'er,
Death and hell behind are cast,
Grief and suffering are no more!

"*Many years ago,*" the minister intoned, "*Richason and Isabelle Yoke tamed the wilderness of this place together. They felled timber, drained swamp, cleared rock, and built a farm. They made a farm, and a home, for their nine children. They made a gathering place, of kindness and hospitality, for their friends and neighbors. From their hard work, and faith, came the bounty they created: milk and cheese and butter from the dairy, meat from the smokehouse, grain from the field, greens from the garden and fruit from the orchard. The pride of this house was to always have enough on hand to feed at least twenty persons.*

"*When two sons of the Yokes, John and Nelson, were called to the Great Cause, the restoration of the Union of our Nation, what did they do? They answered the call. When the men of their companies were furloughed, sick in body, broken in spirit from the misery that is war, where did they go?*

We are told, "Be not forgetful to entertain strangers, for thereby some have entertained angels unaware." Did the Yokes entertain strangers?

"*They did. The soldiers came here, to this farm, to help put up crops, for the pleasure of good companionship and the joy of simple country life, to recover their spirits and restore their souls.*

"*Now, today, the eldest son of this family, John T. Yoke, joins his little sister, Ellen, his father Richason, and his heavenly Father. John was sorely tested, suffering from a disease as mysterious as it was agonizing. He bore it in a manly way, like the soldier he was. At the end, he wanted only to return here, with his wife and his children, to the place of his birth, to be among all those he loved. His mother was here. His brothers, sisters, nieces and nephews, friends and neighbors, were here, in this place that his parents prepared for him.*

"*So must we all prepare places of comfort for each other, just as a place has been prepared for you . . .*"

In the dining room, a long table was loaded with neighborly offerings: cakes and pies, rolls, breads, smoked meat and pickled vegetables, jam and honey. A metal bucket held a nearly melted, precious block of ice, with lemon slices floating in the sugar sweetened water, but despite feeling thirsty,

Georgiana didn't go back in the house when the minister was done. The heat and the crowd were too much to bear.

Jesse Manker, a cousin close to her age, found her a little while later, sitting on the barn swing, and handed her some of the cool lemonade in one of their grandmother's fancy rose-patterned teacups.

"The clear glasses are all used, they can't keep up with washing everything," she said, and Georgiana was grateful for the treat.

They sat quietly for a while, until Jessie said, in the shorthanded way of children, "Well, at least the first part of summer was fun."

Georgiana nodded.

"The peacocks were best," she said. The cousins slept over one night, and the two girls shivered and giggled under their quilts, listening to the weird wails outside, pretending they came from ghosts and not birds.

"Don't forget the doughnuts."

On a Saturday in June, when a dozen children's voices could be heard in the yard, Grandmother Isabelle came from the kitchen carrying a laundry basket filled with the sweet fragrant cakes, so fresh the steam would burn if an eager child bit first instead of breaking them open. She had to laugh as their greedy hands reached in. The whole batch was devoured in a matter of minutes. Amazingly, that same morning the two girls counted fifteen fruit pies on the cooling rack.

"Nothing will ever be as good as those doughnuts," Georgiana said, and then they were quiet again.

"Do you want a turn on the swing?" Georgiana asked after a while, but Jessie heard a call from the house.

"I have to go now," she said. "I'm sorry about your father, Georgiana. Do you know yet where you're going to school?"

"Mother isn't sure yet, but she thinks we can move near her sister in Edinburgh."

"My school starts in three weeks," Jessie said, "but I guess you have time."

"I guess," Georgiana said.

She sat by herself for a long while, thinking, worrying, slowly tracing her finger over and over the delicate curves of the empty cup.

As the visitors packed up their baskets and chairs and re-tethered their sweaty horses, a small chorus of the faithful returned to the grove of trees for a few more hymns. Over a breeze that finally, blessedly arrived, she could just make out the hopeful strains:

> *Change and decay in all around I see,*
> *O Thou who changest not, abide with me!*

THE REVERIE BROKE when Grandmother Isabelle opened her eyes, and miraculously, was lucid enough to recognize her visitor. They spoke of the things Isabelle could remember. The treacherous crossing from Ireland, finally reaching Indiana in the Conestoga wagon. Building the house. Baking fruit pies. Children and grandchildren, jumping from barn swings, finding kittens in the hay, catching frogs in Bean Creek.

Georgiana decided not to mention her forthcoming marriage. In such a declining state, new information would only be confusing to her grandmother, and after an hour, when Isabelle tired and drifted off to sleep again, Georgiana tiptoed out of the room.

Downstairs in the kitchen, when Uncle George poured some hot tea, she recognized the china cup. Her finger traced the delicate handle, curved like a letter formed with perfect penmanship.

"I remember these! How pretty they are."

"Mother always liked roses," he said.

"We spoke for quite a while, and she kissed me goodbye," Georgiana said, and Uncle George thanked her for coming, and offered his congratulations on her engagement.

She had hoped some of the Yoke brothers could join them a few days later for her birthday dinner in Franklin, but it was impossible for Nelson, a high school principal, to leave Indianapolis in the middle of the week. George was consumed by harvest chores and tending to Isabelle, so the only others at the party would be Mary and Johnny, Mary's older sister Nan and her husband, William Drake, and their youngest child, cousin Dolph, a boy of fourteen.

She went alone to meet Henry at the train station, and together they walked the short distance to the hotel. Free of luggage but for one wrapped parcel for her mother, they strolled the long way to the house, enjoying the fine fall weather and brilliant hues of the trees. Typically, Henry had made not one concession to the more informal apparel of a small town, but dressed as if he was on his way to the opera, in a waistcoat and high hat, his gold-topped walking cane held at a jaunty angle.

They passed the house of Dr. Hall on the corner, one of the finest in town, and admired the sturdy red brick buildings of Franklin College. Directly across the street from the campus, on a triangular lot backing up to railroad tracks, stood Mary's small white cottage, nearly hidden by several rows of corn stalks that towered in front of the house. A maze-like path cut through them from the fence gate to the front door.

Inside, Henry took in every detail, the modest but immaculate furnishings, hand-sewn curtains, books prominently displayed. His eyes stopped, and then widened, at the fireplace mantle.

It was like a shrine to Georgiana. Displayed on the shelf was a graduation program book, her diploma and college admission award from Edinburgh High School, the Latin diploma from Danville, her teaching certificate, and an astonishingly amateur oil portrait of her. She was posed stiffly in an unfamiliar, elaborately ruffled blue dress, seated in a tufted, throne-like chair against a heavily curtained backdrop. Georgiana cringed, but Mary exclaimed, "Oh, Dr. Holmes, how do you like it? I think the artist painted her eyes just right."

"Where did she sit for it?" he asked with a perfectly straight face.

"Well, a traveling artist came through town, over in Edinburgh I mean, when her class was graduating high school. For what I felt was a reasonable price, he could take a likeness from a photograph, and paint the face on a background and form already done, you see, which is why it was so reasonable! I thought, with Georgiana leaving for school, and who knows when we would have her back again, it would be so much nicer to have the portrait, with colors, rather than just a photograph to remember her," and she gazed at the portrait with motherly pride.

"Not nearly so beautiful as the original subject, I'm afraid," he replied with admirable diplomacy. Mary and Nan exchanged a delighted glance, but then Johnny and Dolph started blowing kisses at each other, clutching at their hearts and dissolving into laughter, until Georgiana had to tell them to hush up and stop acting so silly.

Henry ignored the boys and presented his gift to Mary, an impressive book, bound in red leather, of sermons by John Wesley, an offering so tasteful, so perfectly appropriate, Georgiana sighed in relief, and any awkwardness about the terrible painting was quickly forgotten.

She wasn't happy when Uncle Drake appeared in his gardener's work clothes, but Henry seemed not to notice, and shook his hand in a friendly manner, and asked questions about agriculture and land values, and gave his full attention to the answers. The geniality continued throughout the meal, one of Mary's best efforts, slices of ham glazed with maple syrup, freshly baked sourdough bread and butter, and of course the corn, put up this summer and made even sweeter by fresh cream from Uncle Drake's cow. Henry praised everything, ate heartily, and soon had everyone laughing with amusing stories of the Fair.

It occurred to Georgiana, watching him, that her fiancé really had a wonderful ability to charm a group of people. After only half an hour in her house, it was almost as if he was the host, and they were the guests, as he looked after their comfort, urging Uncle

Drake to step out for his pipe, and Mary to a rocking chair after the meal.

When he actually started to clear his own plate, and it seemed as if he intended help with the dishes, it was hard to know who was the more alarmed by this extraordinary possibility, Johnny, Dolph and Uncle Drake, or the women of the household. After much teasing and protest it was finally decided that Georgiana and Nan would clean up, Mary and Henry would chat by the fire and get better acquainted, and the rest of the males would escape outside until pie.

"Now, Mary," he said, settling in his chair and patting her hand, "Georgiana has told me something of your late husband's sufferings. What a trial for you! And there was nothing to be done?"

He sat back and let her talk.

"Oh, no, Dr. Holmes, that is, Henry, you cannot imagine how terrible it was. He needed the patience of Job! What would I have done, without my dear girl to help me? In the end, there was nothing to do but give him laudanum. I hated to do it, of course, but he would cry out, and couldn't get any sleep unless he was drugged."

"And this began all the way back in the war?"

"Oh, that's perfectly so, he first got the eczema rash in camp, during the siege in Atlanta. He said all the boys had a skin condition of some sort. Once they got into baths and clean clothes again they healed, all except for John. The mystery was, his disease was so slow to progress. At the end of the war, and even a few years later when I met him, it was only a little patch on his back."

"But if it was really eczema, they should have been able to treat that."

"The doctors had never seen such a case," Mary said, and she listed all the remedies that were tried and failed. Boiling hot compresses, tied tight with rubber bandages. Frictions of potash soap, applied hard. Arsenic.

"They just seemed to make it worse," she said.

Henry, with a slight wrinkle of his nose, murmured, "Yes, I'm not surprised."

Mary went on to describe the persistent red blotches that finally flared into oozing sores and black scabs, fanning out from the chest to the arms, down the legs and then to the feet. The itching grew excruciating, unbearable in hot weather. When the disease finally crawled under his toenails, John had to quit wearing shoes.

"But eczema, even as bad as that, wouldn't kill a man."

"True. The skin disease was the cause of much of his misery, and disfigurement, but the stomach ailment finally finished him," Mary explained. "That started in the war as well, and slowly got worse over time. He couldn't hold in any nourishment, had constant diarrhea. By the last year of his life he ate nothing but boiled rice and oatmeal, at the end, not even that, poor man."

"He must have been constantly dehydrated," the doctor said. "Very hard on the body. Did he finally have heart failure, or a stroke?"

"The Lord only knows, but by that time, he was just a skeleton, except for his stomach that was all swollen. I tell you, Henry, there we were, on the most prosperous farm in the county, and I believe my husband starved to death."

In the kitchen, meanwhile, Aunt Nan and Georgiana rinsed and dried dishes, engaged in companionable discussion, Nan praising the new addition to their family.

She was delighted by how well everything was working out. They had only to get Johnny through school to some sort of trade, and then Mary could rest easy, perhaps take a vacation somewhere if there was money enough?

Georgiana agreed with all these satisfying ideas. She wiped a plate, and considered what variety of flower she might choose for her china pattern.

To let her aunt spend more time with Henry, Georgiana volunteered to round up the boys, and she smiled to herself on the way out the door as she heard Henry say, "Now, Mrs. Drake, I want to hear all about you and Mary. Georgiana said your family was from Illinois. When did you first come to Indiana?"

"Oh, please, just call me Nan. Well, I had to go to work in Edinburgh in '63. But Mary should tell it."

"Oh, no, Nancy, you know all that part better than I do! I need to go and get the pie ready anyway."

Mary got up to return to the kitchen, and let Nancy take over her chair to finish the family history.

"Mary was only fifteen, you see, when our father, Martin Toner, died in the war."

"What a pity, for both Mary and Georgiana to lose a father at such a tender age."

"It was. That's very true. I always felt that gave Mary a special understanding of Georgiana. But our family was large, there were nine of us, and Georgiana was really alone, because Johnny was just a baby, he doesn't remember his father," Nan said.

"Nine children! But no man would be drafted with nine children," Henry said, "how is it possible he was in the war?"

Nan took a deep breath.

"Well, here's how it happened. 1862 looked to be a fine growing season, and most of the neighbors expected huge yields, but the chinch bug came along and ruined our father's corn crop. He lost all his money. So when a neighbor offered a substitution bounty to join the army, he took it.

'The war won't last much longer,' he assured everyone. 'It may even be over by the time I get there'. He lied about his age. He was actually close to fifty, but he put age forty on his form, and they ignored his grey hair.

"He was mustered in at Camp Terry on August 28, 1862. Five days after Christmas, he was dead of disease – he never even saw battle.

"Well, our family's financial situation was desperate. I was twenty-two, the oldest child in the family, so I was put on the train to Edinburgh, with a letter from our mother, asking for a job in our cousin Jacob's grain mill. Jacob Toner was making a fortune providing flour to the Union army, and everyone thanked Heaven he agreed to help us.

"So you see, Henry," Nancy concluded, "our poor Mary sacrificed both a husband *and* a father to the same war!"

"How sad! But it is wonderful to be so close to your sister. So Mary followed you to Edinburgh, and then here to Franklin?"

"Well, partly that," Nancy said. She leaned closer and lowered her voice.

"They came to Edinburgh for the children's schooling when John died. After Georgiana left for college, Mary had to have a long talk with Johnny. She made him promise that if they moved to a town with a bigger high school, with enough boys for a baseball team, that he would try harder. I'm sorry to say, his grades were never what they should be, like Georgiana's. She was always an excellent student. Did you know she passed the teachers examination on the first try? Hardly anyone does that. But Johnny, he would fidget and daydream, and play hooky, and then get the switch!"

"A difficult situation, for any mother," Henry said.

"I should say! Well, our cousin Jacob advised her that she could get a good price for her house there, and buy this one for cash money, and with his help, it worked out."

"I should like to meet him," Henry said, but Nan shook her head.

"He passed away, last year. He was such a clever man. He invented a new milling process, held the patent on it, and built the finest house in Edinburgh. Not always an easy person, but he was good to us, over the years."

From this conversation, Henry easily deduced everything left unsaid: the daily trials as a poor cousin, a dependent, small, constant humiliations, delicate reminders of past generosity. No wonder Georgiana was so ambitious. He pressed Nancy's hand, and thanked her for helping him gain such a clear understanding of his new family.

When Georgiana and the boys returned, Mary was showing the doctor her medicine bottle. She purchased the tonic for occasional attacks of nerves, which, though not nearly so serious as Georgiana's condition, disturbed her enough to seek relief. Henry unstopped it and sniffed the bottle, and held it up to the window.

"I believe this is a temperance household, Mary?"

"Why yes, of course!"

Henry smiled. "Definitely, this product has alcohol in it. Not enough to cause impairment, or anything beyond a minor relaxation of the muscles. Still, it's there."

"That's terrible!" Mary was outraged. "Everyone knows most people don't want alcohol in their system, for any purpose, yet they would sneak it into a bottle! I shall write a letter."

"I can't imagine a letter will do any good," Henry said, "but perhaps you'll allow me to mix up a remedy of my own devising, a formula without spirits but, I do believe, is a good deal more effective, and less dangerous besides."

"Oh! I wouldn't want to impose, but that is very kind, if you really think it is the right thing for me."

"Are you a temperance man yourself, Henry?" Nan asked, as they returned to the table. Mary began slicing peach pie.

"I am not convinced on the legal argument," Henry replied. "I have no personal use, as I've told Georgiana in the past, for either spirits or tobacco. Of the two," and he stopped to smile appreciation for the heaping plate Mary handed him, "of the two vices, from a purely medical point of view, I am actually more opposed to tobacco, particularly in the form of the cigarette. Terrible for the health, especially when started young."

He sent a hard and meaningful look in the direction of the two boys. "Sneaking them in outbuildings, which all young boys try at one time or another, can start a fire, and smoking them can lead to croup, or even whooping cough, in rare cases. Very bad habit, indeed." The adults at the table nodded in solemn agreement, even Uncle Drake, who had just been outside smoking a pipe.

Johnny's mouth fell open with all the outrage of the unjustly accused. He hadn't smoked in months. Anyway, who was this fellow, old as the uncles, dressed up like a king's undertaker, to come in from nowhere and deliver a scolding? He didn't even care about sports, unless you counted bicycle riding, which Johnny certainly did not. It was just like Georgiana to bring home a future brother-in-law who was no fun at all.

Cousin Dolph, had, in fact, recently started a small fire from a cigarette in the outhouse, and just barely got it stamped out in time before it spread. He decided it was best to change the subject, so he cleared his throat, and announced, "Teacher had a contest today, to see who could write the best news story from the inventions at the Fair, about what life will be like in the next century. They were predictions. Mine was the best," which was not exactly true, but did the trick.

"What was your prediction?" Aunt Nan asked.

"Next century, all the buildings, houses and everything, will be built four stories tall. There will be kitchens on the top floor, with an elevator to take people to the different rooms, because electricity will be so cheap everyone will have it," and he pointed a fork triumphantly at his pie, successful in this diversion from the smoking topic. Everyone laughed.

"Why have a kitchen on top? Where would the scraps go, and why would you want to pump water all the way up there?" Georgiana argued.

"It was in the newspaper," Dolph said, holding his ground.

"Our class did that contest too," Johnny said. "We talked all about automobiles."

"He's crazy for automobiles," Georgiana explained to Henry.

"They're a wonder! Some day, they may take the place of trains. When I graduate, I want to make them," but as usual, Johnny was overruled.

"They are an interesting novelty," Henry said, "but far too expensive for the average man. Rail is the thing to get work in. Rail is the cheapest, most efficient transportation there is, and getting better every year."

"A lot of railroads have gone bankrupt this year," Uncle Drake pointed out.

"A temporary setback, that's all. Rail stocks will make a full recovery next year. But perhaps," Henry added, turning to Johnny, "some day automobiles could take the place of a livery, driving people from the station to hotels and such. I can see a possible market for that," but the discussion ended with a general dismissal of the boys' improbable fancies.

The Drakes went home soon after this exchange, with many thanks and good wishes and expressions of pleasure at making Henry's acquaintance. Henry himself left for the hotel at the same time, explaining he had a good deal of paperwork to do. The women shook their heads in wonder at his industriousness.

Georgiana and Mary sat together in the kitchen, sipping tea and reviewing the meal, and decided it was a great success. The food was excellent, even if Mary did say so herself. The company got on very well together, and how fortunate, they agreed, and what a good thing for Johnny, that there would soon be another man in the family.

Johnny and Dolph headed out to throw a ball while there was still daylight.

"That doctor is a real pill," Dolph said, pleased with his joke, but Johnny didn't answer. He gave his full attention to a clump of dry mud he was kicking, hard, down the street, until he reduced it to nothing.

The second week of December, Georgiana sent Henry a telegram, letting him know her grandmother had died, but he didn't receive it in time to attend the funeral. He sent, however, a long and poetic letter of condolence, addressed to the whole family, and a check for fifty dollars to Isabelle's church.

Henry couldn't be there, either, when Uncle Nelson called the family together and read the terms of the will, dividing shares of the farm equally between Isabelle's surviving children and the children of her dead son.

A fire had broken out on the top floor of Henry's hotel – thankfully the floor was empty since the Fair was over, and no one was hurt – but untangling the details of insurance and repairs before his departure, plus wrapping up all his other businesses, would take every bit of his time and attention until Christmas.

The holiday approached, messages flew back and forth – he was down in St. Louis, then southern Illinois, a meeting in Chicago, he would be there soon, but there was a snowstorm, trains were delayed – and he didn't finally appear until the morning after Christmas, bustling and energetic, delighted and relieved to be back in Franklin at last, a cheery tardy Santa, with gifts for everyone.

For Georgiana, it was a lovely gold-and-pearl locket. For Mary, he had a jigsaw puzzle, with a hundred pieces, forming a picture of the Eiffel Tower.

"When we visit Paris, we'll send you a postcard, after we go to the top of this thing," Henry said. "Just imagine what *that* elevator ride is like!" Mary looked alarmed, but Georgiana found the prospect thrilling.

He had a package for Johnny too, which made the boy feel awkward and uncomfortable, since he already decided to hate the man. Henry watched closely as Johnny took the box, marked *Bennington,*

Made in Germany, which opened to reveal twelve marbles, one set of blues and two sets of browns, shiny glass with milky white swirls. Johnny was too grown up to play with marbles, but he could certainly still collect them, and this set was a beauty.

"My partner in Frankfurt recommended them," Henry said. "His boy plays with this kind."

"Thanks, Dr. Holmes, it's a really nice present," Johnny said politely, and Mary gave a silent sigh of relief.

There was another present for Georgiana, a traveler's Bible, inscribed with a beautiful message in Henry's hand: *You are my solace, inspiration and hope.* He really had, she thought, a wonderful talent for selecting the perfect gift.

Henry waited until after dinner. Aunt Nan and Uncle Drake stopped over, and the family was gathered, comfortably with cups, around the fireplace, when he announced his startling news.

"We have to make a change in our plans. We're going to be married in Denver," he said. Georgiana looked at him in astonishment. Why hadn't he told her about this first?

"I must explain," Henry continued. He set down his coffee and stood up before the group, placing a hand on Georgiana's shoulder. "It's all very complicated. This has been quite a month for me. I should own stock in Western Union, for all the telegrams I've sent!

"As you know, my uncle passed away last summer, and left me, his only heir, a property in Fort Worth, Texas. I was notified of the death by letter from his lawyer in Denver, which is where he died. There was a provision, however, which he neglected to tell me at that time, which states that I would have to take his name, Mansfield Howard, in order to inherit.

"I objected, naturally, and consulted my own attorney. However strange, the provision was legally sound and the will could not be broken. If I do not accept, the whole amount is forfeited to the government. Well, what else could I do? Should I sacrifice the launch of my invention, out of pride over a name?"

Heads around the circle nodded. Certainly, no one could be expected to do that.

Georgiana said, "I thought it was your father's brother. Was he not also named Holmes?"

"He changed it, after the quarrel I told you of. It was a way of renouncing the family. I hate to speak ill of him, but the truth is, the whole estrangement was my father's fault. He was a hard man, bitter and unyielding, and I'm sorry to say I have no happy memories of him."

"But how odd, to change a name! I've never heard of such a thing," Mary said.

"Actually, it's more common than you might think. New arrivals to this country, with foreign sounding names, often change them to sound more American. Actors, writers, many professions cause people to use different names. The legal process is not complicated, but it must be posted in the newspaper. If you look at the back of one, in any large city, you'll see such notices."

"Can't you change it here, and get married in Franklin?" Mary said, but Henry shook his head with apparent regret.

"No, the lawyer himself must witness my signature, and have it notarized — no, the best solution is for us to travel out there, work it out with my uncle's lawyer, and get married as soon as the name business is complete."

"But to travel together first —"

"Oh, no, certainly not! I would not permit such a thing without an escort. Fortunately, things have a way of working out. Since I've closed up my Chicago office, all the typists had to seek new employment. My main one, Minnie Williams, has family in Denver, and will go out there at the same time. Some of the other girls may go as well, on a lark, if they don't have jobs by the New Year. So, Georgiana can share a sleeping car with one of them."

Georgiana's head was still spinning at this rapid change of affairs, but now she spoke up.

"Isn't she the brown haired one?" she asked. "The girl who seemed cross that day I visited?"

Henry had a ready reply.

"Oh, don't worry, she has a beau, a serious one, in fact he may already be in Denver, asking her family's permission. And, I'll need someone to take dictation on the train, so it works out well for everyone."

"Still," Mary said, "I would like to have seen Georgiana's wedding."

Georgiana looked down at the floor in embarrassment.

Henry, after a brief, visible hesitation, said, "Well, why not? I can bring you out there, and Johnny too, if you like."

"Oh no, Henry! I hope you don't think I was hinting! I wouldn't dream of putting you to all that expense, and besides, Johnny can't leave school that long. No, you two should go ahead with your plan, and have a wonderful trip, and when you get back, we'll have a lovely party."

Henry beamed at her.

While the company gathered up dishes and put on their coats and hats, Henry took Georgiana aside and murmured in her ear, "Thank you, my dear, for not making a fuss. Your faith in me means everything! I promise you, everything will work out for the best," and she accepted an inviting kiss from him that made her imagination turn to Denver.

Later, in the kitchen, Georgiana said confidentially to Mary, "I have a feeling poor Uncle Nelson is just overwhelmed, with all his responsibilities at the school, his boys, and now everything with Grandmother, too. He got all in a stew when I was in Chicago. Dear man, he thinks he hasn't done enough for us since Father died, can you imagine?"

Mary shook her head in wonder at that, and Georgiana continued.

"So, perhaps it would be best not to mention all this name business to him right now. No need to worry him. Just put the announcement in the Franklin paper, after we're married, with the name Henry Mansfield Howard, and we'll explain it all when we get back."

Mary agreed that this was a good idea.

3

The Everywhere Journey

January — November 1894

HENRY WAS ANGRY, fuming, the only warm thing on the Chicago train platform on this biting cold January day. He had arrived early, to meet Georgiana's train from Indianapolis, and transfer her to the one headed for Denver. Their trunks were already loaded in the baggage car.

But Minnie Williams was nowhere to be found. The train was leaving in less than half an hour. She should have arrived at least an hour ago.

"That flighty girl, why did I trust her to buy her own ticket? Maybe she was confused about our reservation. I'll go talk to the ticket office."

He pulled out his watch, and with a great, annoyed sigh, left Georgiana to shiver on a cold bench just inside the station door, keeping watch in case Miss Williams should still appear.

All the other girls in the office were staying, as it turned out, and only Miss Williams was booked to accompany them. Though she didn't like the prospect of sharing space with that girl, the alternatives were worse — she could travel with Henry, unmarried and without a chaperone, or return home alone. She thought of the newspaper announcement of her engagement, already printed, the marriage announcement cards, already composed, the many warm wishes, already received. She imagined the comments, speculation. Would people think they had quarreled? That the engagement was over? She thought of her mother, and Uncle Nelson, and nearly groaned aloud.

Then suddenly, thankfully, Henry was back, his anger vanished, relief on his face.

"You'll never believe this, but the stupid girl eloped last night!" he said. "She left a message for me in the ticket office. I managed to change your reservation. You'll be sharing a sleeping car with a nice old widow from New York. How's that for a bit of luck?"

Georgiana sighed. "I think, Henry, all in all, it would be best if we don't mention this business about Miss Williams to my mother."

Thanks to recent improvements in train travel, just two days separated Chicago from Denver. Throughout the journey, she only talked to Henry at meals. She appreciated his discretion. No one would imagine they were traveling together. At night she listened to the gentle kitten purr snores of her elderly roommate. During the day she sat by herself and watched the country stretch by the window. Henry immersed himself in work, which he managed to do despite the absence of Miss Williams, until finally she felt a little neglected.

"I do wish," she said, during their final supper on the train, "I knew shorthand or something. I'd like to be of some help to you."

"No wife of mine will work," Henry replied, and then saw her frown.

"But say," and he brightened with an idea. "Here's something you can do." He pulled from his case of papers a leather bound diary, all the pages blank.

"Keep a daily journal of every place we stop," he said. "That would help me immensely. Make note of the hotel, how long we stay, and so on. You may not be an actual secretary, but in our marriage, you will certainly be the social secretary. You may as well start now," and she was delighted with the task, and tucked the diary by her side.

"There may be some working wives in Denver," she said, teasing him. "After all, Colorado women have the vote."

"Don't think too much about that," he said. "We won't be staying long."

But they ended up staying longer than expected.

Henry installed her in a single room at the Brown Palace, and checked himself in at another hotel, for the sake of decency not even telling her where he was staying. He came over for meals, but spent the rest of the time engaged in the struggle to accomplish the name change and finalize the details of his inheritance.

Each day, he told her about one thing after another going wrong.

First, the legal process for the name change was more cumbersome than he expected, so they missed the deadline for the newspaper notice, and had to wait until the following week. Next, the usual notary got sick, and a new one had to be found, and then the new one had a long line of tasks, and so could not notarize the documents until the week after that.

He explained all this with great exasperation, and anxiety for her sake. Georgiana had to reassure him that she was fine, and very self sufficient, and could entertain herself for a few more days.

The Trinity Methodist Episcopal church was just a block away, and easy to find thanks to its tall steeple. She attended the Sunday service by herself. She sipped tea in the atrium-crowned lobby of the grand hotel, where all the tourists gazed up at the magnificent stained glass ceiling, and she chatted with an elderly couple from Indiana. She discovered a public library, housed in a wing of the nearby high school. She studied the latest clothing styles in Godey's magazine, and was amused by the outrageous feminism of a new novel, *Beyond the City*, by Arthur Conan Doyle. She walked around the business district, occasionally stopping at a store, not to buy but to see if any of the new fashions already reached this far west, and compare what they had to the merchandise at Siegel Cooper.

Even in respectable neighborhoods, however, she encountered a disturbing sight. Alarming numbers of vagrants camped in the streets and alleys, ragged men and unkempt women, bundled against the cold by layers of all the clothing they owned, their few spotty possessions behind them all in a heap. They huddled around little fires that policemen repeatedly doused. They hunched on boxes and broken chairs, sometimes extending an empty cup before passing businessmen and shoppers. Bands of truant, wild looking boys ran loose, sometimes brushing right past Georgiana's skirts, and she feared they might be purse-snatchers. One day, she found herself accosted by a dirty waif of a girl no older than six, holding out a wanting hand.

"Can I have some money?" the child said, and Georgiana, startled by this, didn't want to be unkind, so she retrieved a coin from her bag.

At the church she visited, a collection was taken for "silver charity." She had no idea what it meant, but again, not wanting to appear stinting, she made a contribution, and decided to ask Henry about it at their next meal together.

"Colorado got the worst of last year's recession. The government stopped buying silver," he explained, "so the prices dropped by more than half. The mine owners went bankrupt, and threw thousands of miners out of work."

She nodded her head, but really felt quite stupid. Of course she heard there was a political argument over silver, but it made no sense to her until now. Everyone she knew in Chicago just ignored the recession during the Fair.

"It won't bother us, though," he said. "My businesses are solid, and investors will be looking for money-saving devices like my machine."

She told him about the begging ragamuffin.

"She was all alone, at such a young age! I felt quite sorry for her."

Henry reached for her hand.

"You are so good, to take pity on poor creatures, but I assure you, she wasn't alone. There was an adult nearby, watching her performance, and waiting to collect the proceeds! It's sad, but in every city there are such people," and to keep her from feeling distress, he changed the subject, and turned the conversation to the happy prospect of their impending marriage, which would happen, finally, on the 17th of January.

It was an evening wedding. The carriage ride was long, a full two miles from the hotel to the small Fifth Avenue Methodist Episcopal Church, but the weather was unusually warm, so she was not uncomfortable. Henry explained he chose this more out-of-the-way location because his uncle's lawyer belonged to this church, and he was trying in every way to be agreeable.

Reverend Wilcox was a well-established figure in the Denver Methodist community, and he chatted with Georgiana on various issues for so long, Henry finally grew impatient.

The ceremony was simple and brief. The two employees of the household, Mr. Osenbaugh and Mrs. Anderson, served as witnesses. Afterwards they had a short prayer, a lemonade toast, and before long they were back in the carriage.

Now, time to return to the hotel together, time for their wedding night, and the long awaited, customary unlacing.

Henry showed great restraint, and did not exercise any undue pressure on her. He displayed such consideration for her modesty and her dignity, that later she was able to say she found the whole experience altogether joyful. He combed her long golden hair with his fingers, and assured her he felt the same way.

On the train to Fort Worth, she started to comprehend how completely Henry's manner of living diverged from that of the rest of the world. The man just didn't seem to need sleep. He never stayed in their bed for long.

If she woke briefly in the night, from a sudden motion or screech of the brakes, she could watch him, with one small light on, hunched over papers, or furiously writing, or restlessly pacing the three steps of the tiny compartment. Yet he rarely seemed tired. His energy was bottomless, his cheerful optimism boundless. He worked, isolated, feverishly, for hours at a time, and then stopped, suddenly, like a galloping animal halted at the edge of a cliff.

Then all was conversation, relaxation, jokes, as if the mad rush of work did not exist. Then she had his full attention.

How disorienting for her, and how strangely exhilarating, to be without an occupation, without any obligation but marriage, the only structure of their day dictated by the hours of the dining car. To lounge about in full daylight, wearing only a nightgown, in close company with a man, felt wanton, and she had to remind herself that it was all right, even expected, now that she was married, and on her honeymoon journey, far from the jurisdiction of home.

The train stopped for a couple of hours at a station half a day out of Fort Worth, and Henry got off to send some telegrams, notifying his business contacts that they'd be arriving soon. When he got back he shut their door with a hard bang, letting her know he was upset.

"I got a message from my uncle's assistant in Fort Worth," he said. "He gave me bad news. Some squatters, a gang of very tough men, have taken possession of my uncle's ranch."

"Why, that's terrible! What will you do? Can you notify the law?"

He considered, staring at her intently.

"There's not much law in Fort Worth, I'm given to understand. I have another idea. I say we trick them. When we get to town, we won't go by Mansfield Howard, for of course they'd recognize that name. I'll use an alias, scout around, and find out what they're up to."

"Henry," she said, "I think that sounds dangerous. I think you need to send a message to your lawyer in Denver."

"I certainly will. How smart of you! But he can't do much from a distance. I need to get some inside help on this, without these outlaws' knowledge."

He raised his finger, as if he just had an idea.

"From this moment, everywhere in Fort Worth we'll give our names as Mr. and Mrs. Pratt. Just until I figure out what's happening on the property."

"But I was just getting used to Howard! Are you really sure we need to do this? It just feels so strange to me, having three different names in one week!"

He looked hurt.

"I thought you had more faith in my judgment."

"Of course I have faith in you, but—"

He raised his voice, just a bit.

"You might show a little more understanding. These fellows are certainly armed. I'm only thinking of my safety, and yours!"

"Oh, dear, I'm so sorry. Of course you're right. We'll do whatever you say, we'll do whatever you think is necessary."

That seemed to mollify him. He glanced down at his pocket watch, and then, smiling, he held out his arms, full of forgiveness.

"I think a lot of things are necessary. Come on over here, Mrs. Pratt."

HER FIRST IMPRESSION of Fort Worth was a jumble of banging construction as their luggage was loaded onto a wagon that was hitched to the back of their carriage. They moved out slowly through traffic. She looked out the window of the passenger seat at a treeless maze of mostly two and three story buildings, and pulled her traveling veil close over her face against the dust hovering around every building site.

This must be just as Chicago was twenty years before the Great Fire, Georgiana thought, dirty streets still largely unpaved, unimproved, disorganized. A few structures boasted ornate clock towers, and at the far end of Main Street a nearly completed domed courthouse loomed, but mostly there were the plain facades found in any small town. At least there was a substantial use of brick, but Fort Worth's Main Street was not nearly as wide as Chicago's State Street. Trolley tracks rolled right down the middle, leaving hardly enough room on either side for two wagons to pass each other. Telegraph poles lined the sidewalks, their single wires forming a spindly canopy over the crowded street.

Each aspect that discouraged her, however, animated Henry. He looked approvingly at the crews of men, perched on scaffolding at nearly every other building, sawing and pounding, hoisting timbers, laying rows of brick.

"Here's progress, this is what prosperity looks like," he said, "with activity like this, you can't help but make money," and he squeezed her hand. He pointed out, too, the excellent weather for development. "There's very likely a blizzard in Chicago right now, and below zero, and here we are in bright sunshine and easily sixty degrees. There is no idle season here," and she had to admit the winter would be more easily passed in such a mild climate.

Then his mood changed, in a flash, to anger.

"Don't go there," he shouted to the cab driver. The man looked back, noticed Georgiana, and nodded his head. From Rusk Street he made a turn back to Main, but not before she saw through her veil the spectacle of women in brightly colored dresses, leaning out of windows or lounging casually in front of dilapidated buildings.

"Why so close to the rail station?" Henry demanded. "That's no sight for a respectable lady just come in to town," but the driver just shrugged his shoulders.

"The Acre was there before the railroad," he replied, and not another word was said until they reached their hotel.

For a town supposedly on the way up, the hotel was remarkably shabby. A diamondback rattlesnake lay coiled in the front yard, shot dead that very morning. The stairs to the front door creaked dangerously. Strips of faded wallpaper peeled away from corners. There was indoor plumbing, but it wasn't at all nice.

Tired out from the long train ride, Georgiana went to bed after minimal unpacking, and didn't even hear Henry go out.

He was gone the next morning, too. A note left on the desk told her he had business to see to, and she should go downstairs and meet the landlady who would fix her breakfast.

Unlike her hotel, the landlady was reassuring. A friendly woman, plump and maternal, she took one look at Georgiana and announced she needed a Texas-style breakfast, which meant a generous amount of food and hospitality. Georgiana felt her spirits rise as she ate, and the landlady watched with approval while drinking her own coffee.

How pleasant to relax with this kindly woman. It had been several weeks, now that she thought of it, since she had an extended conversation with anyone except Henry.

"What does your husband do, Mrs. Pratt?" the landlady asked, while refilling her cup, and Georgiana felt a jolt. She still had to get used to hearing herself called by her newest name. She reviewed in her mind the long list of Henry's accomplishments.

"He has many enterprises," she said. "He's a medical man, and has a pharmacy business, and several real estate interests. We're here to claim a property he inherited, and then we'll travel through the country as he develops capital for an office machine of his own invention. Next year we go to Germany to lease the factory where it will be built."

She paused, thinking how very impressive this must all sound to a keeper of a small hotel, out here in the western wilderness. She must be careful not to sound bragging, and she delicately wiped her mouth.

"Of course, not every speculation can be a success. I guess he wants to try his hand at many things while he's still young, and then settle into one or the other later on."

"How romantic, a handsome young couple like you, to travel the world!" the landlady said, and Georgiana warmed to her even more.

"I'll be on my own much of the time, he is so busy. I was hoping there would be a library here."

"Well, there will be soon, it's one of the projects the ladies of Fort Worth have wanted more than anything for some years. It's just getting started, and won't be finished for a while."

"That is a fine improvement," Georgiana said.

"Oh, our Fort Worth ladies are quite something. They wrote to Mr. Carnegie, and he promised fifty thousand dollars for the library for us, but we must also raise a sum to maintain it. The ladies held sales, cakewalks and dances and teas and so on, but were still short the money. So Mrs. Keeler started the cigar campaign."

"Cigar campaign?"

The woman laughed.

"They went right up to any man on the street, whether they knew him or not, just right up to his face, if he was smoking a cigar, and demanded a contribution for the library at the price of the cigar he was smoking! 'Is that cigar more valuable than a literate child?' they would say, and shamed them right into it, or made them laugh at their gall, and so they collected what was needed."

"I love that," Georgiana said. "That's even better than saloon vigils."

"Saloon vigils won't go far in Fort Worth," the woman said, with a roll of her eyes. "We can't even enforce Sunday closings."

"Speaking of Sunday," Georgiana said, "can you tell me if there is a Methodist church in the area?"

"We're mostly Baptist here," the landlady said, "but yes, there is Southern Methodist, Northern Methodist, and the Methodist Episcopalian Negro, but I guess you'll want the Northern Methodist," and she wrote it down for Georgiana to give to Henry, so he would know where to take her on Sunday morning.

Henry didn't like the hotel either, and when he came back, announced he found a proper place for a honeymoon. They moved the next afternoon to the Arlington Inn, a luxurious resort four miles from town. There was no problem getting a suite of rooms for an extended stay at a very good price. Business outside of town was slow, still hurt by the recession, and there were hardly any other guests.

Even after she was fully rested and started to wake earlier, Henry was gone before she got up. He sometimes dashed back to join her for a lunch, other days he left a note saying he would not be back until dark. On those late days he was apologetic, worried that she might be bored, and always brought a present of jewelry or flowers. One night he brought an armload of books that he mail-ordered for a surprise, a few light novels and foreign travel guides, and a textbook of German language instruction.

"You'll need to converse with the other wives, once we get there. I'll be depending on you to sort out our invitations," he said.

So what would become the solitary, leisurely routine of her married life was set that first week in Texas.

Her day began with a light breakfast alone, then a stroll around the landscaped grounds of the resort. She sat by the large lobby windows overlooking the garden and read the Bible, then a chapter in one of the novels, wrote postcards and letters, studied German, and waited for Henry to return for lunch or dinner, bringing news of his accomplishments, setbacks, hopes and plans, for her to encourage and applaud. In the evening he spent time with her, sweet and attentive, but after she went to bed he returned to work, spreading out papers and letters, maps and train schedules, real estate contracts and insurance forms.

This must be what all wives of geniuses went through, she told herself. The great musicians, the poets, scientists, entrepreneurs, all had behind them a woman like her, who was patient and understanding, who could see beyond the present, to the gifts and accomplishments the world did not yet recognize. She told herself with certainty that in the future, this temporary isolation would be richly rewarded.

One afternoon something out of the ordinary happened. A stranger came to their door, a tall, rough looking fellow, with a gaunt, stubbly face and close-set, unfocused eyes. He startled her by asking for Dr. Holmes.

"The doctor isn't here," Georgiana said, holding firmly to the doorknob. "I'll take a message for him."

"Mr. Lyman," the person said, and she caught a whiff of his breath before he turned away.

"Henry," she said, before he had a chance to remove his coat, "a Mr. Lyman was here, asking for you as Holmes. Who is he?"

"A man I know from Chicago."

"Are you doing business with him here? He seems like a very wrong sort."

"He knows some people I need to complete a deal, unfortunately."

"Why," she continued, saving the most outrageous for last, "does he reek of alcohol in the middle of the day?"

"Because he's a drunk," Henry said, and the conversation was over.

Although they were now far from town, she still planned to go to church on Sunday.

"That's fine, I have a meeting anyway," Henry said. She already decided to not make an issue just yet about his lack of attendance, but this was a little too much.

"You can't do business on the Sabbath," she said, as she rode next to him in a rented buggy, but he replied while not strictly working, he needed to lunch with a man who was leaving town the next day. Connections, he pointed out, were vital to getting established. His new plan, until the squatters were removed, was to leverage the cost of a town property, improve it for quick resale, and come away with enough profit for the Germany trip.

"Yet," Georgiana said logically, "what better place to form respectable connections in a new town than at church?"

"That shall be your job, my dear," he replied, "as the social head of our household, you must meet some nice people, and tell me all about them," and with that he handed her down and drove away, leaving her to forge ahead alone.

That was all right. She wasn't shy, especially in this familiar setting. When the time came, Henry would be equally comfortable and comforted, she thought. He would eventually turn his remarkable talents to aid the prosperity of their chosen church home, and this happy vision carried her serenely, confidently, to the tea table for the social hour.

She introduced herself as a visitor to the minister, and he introduced her in turn to a quartet of ladies, older than herself, finely dressed and elaborately hatted. They were all earnest women, active in local causes. She congratulated them on the library campaign, and added, "I understand the saloon laws are weak here. Is temperance not gaining ground, as it is back east?"

This, it seemed, was a sore subject. All four grimaced, and put forth their collective outrage.

"Too many interests are allied against it," said one, and the others nodded. "For years, Fort Worth has been known as a savage place, where the cowboys came to gamble and drink and fight, and so on. The corruption became embedded, the politicians, the police collecting bribes, the young sons of even the good families, here and as far as Dallas, all taking part. It's better now, but there is still so much to be done."

"The opposition just laughs at our attempts," another added. "Good Heavens, the first jail they built here, they neglected to put a lock on the door."

They all shook their heads at this, and the woman continued.

"There was a Methodist church, St. Paul's, in the vicinity of the Acre, and when they moved out, it became a saloon, but just to mock us they kept the name of St. Paul!"

"The Acre?" Georgiana was puzzled. She kept hearing this name.

"It's called Hell's Half Acre," the tallest woman grimly allowed this swear to pass her lips, "though it now takes up more than two acres of the town. It is a section where every form of vice is nurtured, and goes on seven days a week, twenty-four hours a day."

"There are mixed races in the Acre," said the first, confidentially. "There are dope fiends, Mrs. Pratt, among the unfortunate females who populate these streets. There are suicides of girls by morphine every week!"

"Who would have imagined the ideals of the pioneers, coming to civilize the west, would be so debased?" Georgiana said, thinking of the horror her grandparents would have felt, had they known of such things, and the ladies nodded. On that note of agreement, three of them turned back for tea and cookies, and Georgiana continued to converse with the first.

"You do say things are better now, there has been improvement and progress, do you attribute that to an influx of good people to the area?"

"There is that, of course, with our growth in population, more families and so on, and then, certain events have made even the worst of the rabble realize they cannot continue on as they have."

"Certain events?" Georgiana pressed, thinking optimistically that a particularly effective revival took place, but that hope was quickly dashed.

"There was a murder, Mrs. Pratt. Not just the random shootings of the cowboys, but one, of a girl, that was so horrible, so shocking, even the residents of the Acre cried out for justice."

"My goodness." Georgiana felt a chill, as the woman glanced about, then lowered her voice.

"A woman of the streets, her name was Sally, that's the only name she was known by. Mrs. Pratt, she was crucified!"

Georgiana wondered if her informant was touched in the head. To use such a term, while sipping tea at a church social hour, seemed a particularly bizarre form of blasphemy.

"I know," the woman went on, "it sounds incredible, but it really happened, about three years ago. She was found in the morning, nailed up, nails right through her hands, to the door of an outhouse in the Acre. No one was caught, or charged, or even suspected. Everyone who lives there, or anywhere near Fort Worth for that matter, was terrified. There was no way to know, was it a stranger who just passed through? Was it someone here, in our midst? What kind of a person could do such a strange and terrible act, such violence against a woman? A lot of the girls up and left, we were told, and after that, we had some success with enforcement of law and order. Everyone, you might say, sobered up."

She finished her tea, and stared for a moment out the window, at the calm street, where carriages ambled by and children, freshly released from Sunday school, hopped and jostled and nibbled cookies.

Georgiana was speechless. Her bright optimism of the early day gave way to intense distress. She wanted only for Henry to arrive, to take her back to the hotel. When he finally did come, she was silent the whole way back, until they were in their room, and then, tearfully, she told him what she learned.

Henry consoled her, reasoning that nothing else of the kind had happened since, so some mad vagrant was likely responsible. Probably a thousand miles away, if he was even still alive. Such things did not happen, after all, he said, to respectable people, who were not out looking for trouble.

"I'm nervous out here in the country. I need to be near people, if you are to be gone so much. Please, please, find a safe place in town," and she cried some more, and her heart raced so fast she lost her breath.

Henry saw an opening, and took it.

"That's fine, I'd like to be closer in now too, since I've started a new building project. But Georgiana, I see no reason to mix too much with these people. If you want to go to church, you can, but there's no point in putting down roots in a place we'll be leaving soon anyway. If we're back in town, I don't want you wandering around on your own. Will you promise me?"

Judge Sam Hunter always checked the references of potential tenants for the rooms he and his wife rented out, and the handsome, well-to-do young couple passed muster right away. They were from Chicago, recently married. An investor with large holdings in the east, the husband opened up an impressive bank account in Fort Worth while touring the country, looking for worthwhile projects, and was particularly impressed with the potential here in Texas.

Judge Hunter and his wife were quite taken with Mrs. Pratt, a lovely, demure girl, with the kind of dignified manners so admirable in a woman.

The Judge didn't care so much for the husband, a snob in his opinion. He didn't like his manner, from the first day, towards Mrs. Hunter.

"Will you be eating with the family, Dr. Pratt?" his wife asked, but no, she was informed, quite abruptly, they would be taking their meals at a restaurant across the street.

"He's too good for family style suppers? He thinks restaurant cooking is better than yours?"

"You can hardly blame them," Mrs. Hunter said. "They're obviously so much in love, why should they want anyone else's company?"

"Even so," the Judge replied. "She seems so sweet, and he scowls all the time."

"I think it may be a runaway match," his wife said. "They certainly want their privacy."

"Just so they pay the rent in cash," her husband said.

The Pratt couple stayed only a month, and then the wife informed Mrs. Hunter they would be moving to an apartment above the millinery shop. Light housekeeping, she explained, would be a bit more economical for them, for the duration of their stay.

"Oh, I understand perfectly, but we'll miss you." She really meant it. "Please do come back and visit, before you leave town," and Georgiana promised that she would. But to Mrs. Hunter's surprise, she never did see Mrs. Pratt again.

Later that spring, as Judge Hunter stood on his wide porch, smoking a cigar with one of the tenants after dinner, he heard the first of many rumors about the Pratt couple.

"They left town in a hurry," the man was saying, "and there were debts, big ones. He left his building only half done, and there's a big mess surrounding the title on his property. A Texas girl named Minnie Williams signed it over to his agent, but there was no proper transfer recorded."

"I never liked him," the Judge said.

"They were pretty free spenders. Got a lot of credit. It's what you want, to grow the town, rich folks from back east, coming in and investing, but I don't think they were the real article."

"She didn't have anything to do with it, of that I'm certain," Judge Hunter said. He took a long puff, then sat back and admired his rings of smoke that drifted out over the porch railing.

"You may be prejudiced. You always kind of liked her, I think. Maybe that's why you didn't like him, or why he didn't like you!" the tenant teased, but the Judge didn't respond. The tenant glanced in towards the kitchen, making sure Mrs. Hunter was out of earshot.

"Come on, Sam, admit it."

Judge Hunter didn't take the bait, but looked at him with great seriousness.

"Mrs. Pratt *is* one of the most beautiful women I ever saw in my life. But it's not just that. There's something about her, something warm, special. You can't turn away from her, when she's in the room. I can't say just exactly what it was," and now he paused, seeing that light, youthful figure, the fresh, clear complexion, the golden hair. Those huge eyes, filled with optimism and hope.

"Hers is a face that, once you've see it, you always remember it. I will never forget that girl," he said, "not as long as I live."

———

THE ADVENTURE IN Fort Worth ended abruptly. One afternoon in May, Henry strode in their hotel room, jittery and excited.

"Can you get us packed, right away? I need to be on the train tonight," and laughed at her astonishment.

"I have a great opportunity in St. Louis, a fellow wants me to partner in a pharmacy, similar to my shop in Chicago. While there, I can work on several investors for the copier, but I need to get there right away, or he'll sell the partnership to someone else."

"What about your building, and everything, here?" she asked, but he was looking forward to that question, so he could share his next triumph.

"Sold!" he declared, opening his leather case to display a breathtaking stack of cash bills. He enjoyed the look on her face, and then explained.

"I traded the deed to the ranch for the city lot. The improvement on the lot doubled its value, and now the squatter is the bank's problem," and with that, he whirled back out again, a busy cyclone, leaving her to get the trunks full as fast as she could. He was gone before she had time to ask if they could now go back to being Howard instead of Pratt.

She was shocked when Mr. Lyman resurfaced, lurching down the aisle of the train on the journey to St. Louis, and greeting Henry as if he was expected. They went to the smoking car together. When Henry returned, she told him firmly that she didn't think Mr. Lyman was respectable and they should not socialize with such a person, which only seemed to amuse him. The man was much better, Henry reassured her, in fact, he had been using Henry's own patent alcohol cure to great effect.

"Aren't you the one who believes in redeeming drinkers?" he said, teasing her, but sensing she was really upset, he took her hand and squeezed it. "Please don't worry about him, Georgiana. After our business is complete, we'll never have to see him again."

She grew increasingly nervous, and in St. Louis had an attack of her eye condition, and a violent headache. She pulled the curtains against the bright sun, pressed warm cloths over her eyes, remained in bed, and conjured up wild fancies. She worried that in this unattractive state, Henry's affection for her might wane, that his thoughts could stray back to a different woman, that her listless reliance on him would prove a burden.

But in fact, her helplessness brought out his most tender attentions. He laid out her nightgown, and drew her bath, and pressed his expert fingers against her temples, around her head, down her neck. He brushed out her hair, slowly, almost reverently. One night, he pulled out the strands from her brush, twisted them together and coiled them in a tight circle around his little finger. He pulled off the golden ring of her hair and placed it in a tiny gold-and-jet locket on his watch chain.

"How sentimental you are," she murmured, sleepy from medicine, and Henry smiled.

"What man wouldn't be, when he has a wife like you," he said.

When she was well enough to pay attention, Henry reported that the new drug store partnership was proceeding remarkably quickly, to be finalized in late June, and he had scheduled some promising meetings with investors. All his plans were working out perfectly, he assured her, and from the confines of their room, it never even occurred to her that he might be dead wrong.

Disaster struck on the 19th of July. Henry was away the whole day, then the whole evening, when a telegram arrived. *"Delayed on business all night don't worry"* which of course made her worry. It was sent from within the city, so why would he not just stop back and tell her himself? He never came home that night, and when she heard a sound next morning she jumped up from bed, pulled a shawl over her gown, and prepared to rush to his arms and demand to know what happened.

But it wasn't Henry. A messenger boy was standing outside the door.

"Mrs. Howard?" he said. "I'm so sorry, I knocked, but perhaps you didn't hear me. I apologize for coming so early, I have a message from your husband."

"Where is he? What is the matter?"

He handed her the paper, averting his eyes, and left without waiting for a tip.

She gripped her shawl tight around her body, heart pounding in advance of bad news.

The letter was indeed from Henry, sent from the police station. There had been a great misunderstanding, she was not to worry, but to follow his instructions exactly, and he would be back with her in a matter of hours. She should remove a certain amount of cash from an envelope in his desk, and take it to the office of a lawyer, Mr. Jeptha Howe, who would use the money to furnish bail. She was to deliver it, count it out, and obtain a receipt. She should answer any of his questions as accurately as possible, then return to their room and wait for him. She shouldn't talk to anyone but Mr. Howe.

It was a slow moving nightmare. Jeptha Howe turned out to be a baby faced little man, possibly even younger than she, barely old enough to shave. It seemed inconceivable that he could sort out this ridiculous situation.

"Please," she said. "Please, tell me what this is all about."

"Your husband has a powerful enemy, Mrs. Howard." The youth gazed at her impassively. "There is a dispute over a property in Fort Worth, and our opponent means to win it."

"But he sold that property!"

"The title to it is still unresolved, therefore the plaintiff maintains that the sale was not valid. However, your husband used the proceeds of that sale to purchase a drug store here in St. Louis. The sellers of the drug store were refused payment on their check, until the bank in Fort Worth clears the sale there."

"So Henry should not have bought the drug store? Did he break the law?"

The lawyer shrugged. "Let's say he bent it. He may have acted in good faith, but certainly, a little prematurely. It will take some effort to get him extricated, and much depends on how far his opponent is willing to go. There seems to be some very bad blood involved here, this Fort Worth fellow is out for more than money, but also some kind of revenge. A very dangerous character, so you and your husband must act with great discretion."

Georgiana took a deep breath to calm her quaking nerves, and nodded.

"Just tell me what to do, Mr. Howe."

"I will, Mrs. Howard. Did you bring the money?"

Ten days later, Georgiana and Henry sat, silently facing each other, in matching chairs by the window. She felt exhausted, and wondered how he could remain so energetic, so strangely excited, after all they had just been through together. Release from prison, she surmised, must bring a relieved sort of exhilaration, blotting out the shame and stress. How prophetic Henry had been, back in Chicago, warning her about official corruption, only to find himself a victim of it!

He drummed his fingers, his eyes on the ceiling, for a long while, then abruptly, put his hands on her knees and looked with great tenderness at her face.

"What would I have done without you? How splendid you were, so decisive and businesslike! Whoever says women can't manage things is a fool! How can I ever thank you, Georgiana?"

He was right; she did rise to the occasion. Once her sense of justice was outraged, she carried herself through the whole ordeal with aloof dignity, answering questions with curt precision, staring icicles at anyone who questioned Henry's innocence.

"All I did was what you and Mr. Howe told me to do. But I thought I would die when that attorney started questioning me! That, and men looking at me, was the worst part, once I knew you were safe, of course."

"Well, it's ended, and you managed everything perfectly. And now, we must talk of what to do next. What our next move will be. We can't be too careful, you know."

"What do you mean? Isn't it over, with this Fort Worth man, and all those terrible lies he told? Mr. Howe straightened everything out."

He didn't answer directly, but looked back at the ceiling.

"I must get to Chicago, right away. There are papers in Englewood I need, and other meetings." He stopped. "Georgiana, I want you to take a few days, apart from me. I want you to rest up, forget this business. Go off by yourself for a while. You need it, my dear." He stared at her, with a meaningful look she couldn't quite grasp.

"Why, Henry, surely that's not necessary! I'll be fine once we get to Chicago, we'll go to a quiet hotel, and I'll rest while you work. Why should this trip be any different?"

"My trouble may not be over, not by a long shot. This man is past anything I imagined, vindictive, beyond any normal business competition. He's ruthless, and determined, he thought he won this round and is probably angry that he lost it. There's just no telling what he might do."

"You mean you think you're still in danger? Can't you notify the police?"

"After what they just did to me? Not likely! And who knows which ones are still working with him? I'm not saying anything will happen. I'm just saying I'd feel better if you took a few days for yourself, to rest up, and we'll meet later, in Philadelphia, where we're not known, and things will be a little calmer."

"I can still go to Chicago, and stay with friends. That way I'll be nearby, in case you need me again."

"And who would that be? Your college friends are all gone home. You can't ask your uncle, he would think there was something wrong between us, and then it would get back to your family. We wouldn't want, Heaven forbid, to start rumors in that direction!"

"Well, no, I do see your point. Maybe I could stay with Mary Ellen."

For just a moment, she envisioned the bustling store, the bright, colorful rows of merchandise, the cheerful camaraderie of the lunchroom.

It wasn't what he wanted to hear. She could see it in the tightening of his mouth, the sudden stiffening of his shoulders. She could tell he was annoyed with her, questioning his authority without even fully hearing him out. In the very back of her mind, a jealous inkling nagged, was one of his business meetings with the woman in Wilmette?

Henry's voice turned low and chilly.

"This friend of yours, this Mary Ellen, she is still working?"

Georgiana studied her fingernails.

"She works in the Sewing department."

"And her husband, what does he do?"

"He, actually, I'm not sure at the moment, but he does construction work, different jobs, building things . . ."

"He's an Irish day laborer," Henry said. "Like any fellow who works on my buildings. Georgiana, you must understand, I can't allow it. You're a married woman, married to a doctor. Surely you can see how unsuitable it would be to stay overnight, alone, in the home of a workingman. Do you imagine their household is dry? Have they even a place of their own, or do they live in a boardinghouse?"

Of course he was right.

"I'm sorry, Henry, I do see your point. Maybe I should just go to Franklin, and see my mother. I can wait there until you send for me," though she hated the thought of returning to Franklin without Henry.

He didn't care for that idea either.

"She might wonder if something's wrong. It's vital, it goes without saying, that no word of this St. Louis business should ever get to Indiana."

She pictured Uncle Nelson's disappointed face, and shuddered.

"The idea of my troubles causing worry in the family — I just can't have that. No, there must be some other place for a holiday, a resort perhaps, something like the Arlington. Don't worry about the expense, after all you've been through, you deserve a lovely vacation. We must think of something else."

She pondered this for a minute.

"Up north of Chicago, there is that resort, with the Methodist camp. Lake Bluff. Lots of people from the Methodist Corner go there in the summer, and one girl I know, Sarah Jenkins, her parents have a home there. I think her father is in charge of the temperance program. She always urged me to visit. There's a Chautauqua, and a tabernacle. Just by the lake, it should be a relief from the heat. What about that?"

Now he smiled.

"That sounds fine. Do you have her address? You should write tonight, let them know you're coming, say you've been ill and you need a rest for your health, which is actually quite true. I'll talk to the desk clerk downstairs about sending a wire. Very good, very good . . ."

Henry rose and got writing paper from the desk, ever efficient, back to business. She went to the bed and leaned against the pillows, feeling a little relaxation for the first time in two weeks. She deliberately put her suspicion about Wilmette far from her mind. What was she thinking, when all he cared about was her welfare and her health? She felt ashamed of herself.

"Henry," she said, after a while, "I do appreciate this. It's so like you to be thinking of me, after all you have on your mind. I know it's just what I need."

He looked up.

"I bet they'll have lectures up there, to go along with all the hymn singing. That'll be a fine entertainment for you! And if you get lucky, I mean to say very lucky, maybe Frances Willard herself will be giving the talk."

"Oh, you," she said, laughing, relieved to know everything between them was fine again, and she threw a pillow at his head, knowing it would bring him over to her.

THE VISIT TO the charming village was delightful, and afterwards she felt even more grateful to Henry for suggesting the brief holiday.

Sarah met her at the train spur, and they walked a short distance to the cottage. An aroma of warm sweet baking greeted them at the door, reminding her for all the world of those laundry baskets full of her grandmother's doughnuts.

"Sugar cookies," Mrs. Jenkins explained. "The Deaconess took in half a dozen orphans last spring. She has her hands full now! We're all pitching in," and Georgiana gladly donned an apron and helped to roll out the dough and pack the cookies after they cooled.

Her friend always referred to her Lake Bluff home as a cottage, but it was rather more than that, a year round house, two stories high under a steeply pitched roof decorated with gingerbread trim. Protective mosquito netting draped a white-pillared porch that caught cool winds from the north, west, and most importantly, from the east, off of Lake Michigan.

The house sat along a winding road, bordered by woods and a steep ravine. A shallow stream wandered along the ravine's bottom, barely touched by dappled sunshine. From the porch they could hear children playing below, and their squeals sounded like long-ago summers on the farm with her cousins, wading and splashing in Bean Creek.

The day was hot, almost ninety degrees, but between the lake breeze and deep shade it felt comfortable, even after baking. Thick foliage of great elms and oaks formed a sheltering arch to the middle of the street, eliminating all danger of sunburn, and so they strolled bareheaded, laughing and swinging their baskets of treats for the orphans. Scattered chinks of sunlit sky flickered above, like small blue rips in a great green awning.

They did take their hats, and sun umbrellas too, for their afternoon drive the next day. The buggy was open and they intended to go a long way. Mrs. Jenkins and Sarah took turns holding the reins, so one of them could sit by Georgiana and point out the sights. The road could not run straight, they explained, because it had to wind around the network of deep ravines that stretched several miles to the south.

They followed its curves, passing by the grand mansions of Lake Forest, and for each there was a history her hostesses eagerly shared, which Chicago millionaire built this or that one, what family provided funds for the beautiful Presbyterian church, and the fine buildings of Lake Forest College, who gave the most magnificent teas and parties to benefit all their worthy charities.

"Of course, the rich girls in these houses are always under watch by the newspapers, in case they slip up," Sarah said, but her mother protested at this.

"They have to set an example, what's wrong with that? It's their duty. Someone has to be the leader of Society, after all," and that made perfect sense to Georgiana.

Their destination was the recently constructed Fort Sheridan, and they laughed that the great general had both the fort and the road named after him. Other buggies full of tourists were there, too, circling the parade grounds, admiring the huge tower and the sturdy, greenish-gray brick buildings, setting out picnics in the nearby woods.

"They say they built the fort to protect us from the anarchists," Sarah said, as she unwrapped a sandwich. "But I think we're far too rustic up here, why would they bother to attack us?"

"Was your husband ever a military man, Mrs. Howard?" Mrs. Jenkins asked, and Georgiana was startled for a moment. She hadn't thought about Henry since she got here, and her forgetfulness made her feel a little guilty.

"No," she said, "he went directly to medical college, then into business."

She took a bite of her sandwich, and returned to the anarchists.

"It's so quiet and peaceful up here, I'm sure you have nothing to worry about."

"Well," Mrs. Jenkins said, "if you think it's quiet, you should have heard it last week, when the Salvation Army took over the tabernacle. Whooping and hollering and drumming, day and night! All the neighbors were bothered, let me tell you!"

"It was mighty lively on the Fourth of July, Georgiana," Sarah added. "We had such fun, the biggest picnic you can imagine, swimming and boat races, and a band, and fireworks. I wish you had been here. Everyone around here just loves the Fourth of July!"

"I wish I had too," Georgiana said. "I can't wait to write to Mother, and tell her all about this place. Maybe I could bring her to visit sometime – I know she'd love to see the tabernacle."

"Many who visit end up wanting to stay," Mrs. Jenkins said. "Our little village is a like a sanctuary, a refuge from the evils of the city. That's why they send the orphans up here."

On the last evening of her visit, as they ambled past the Hotel Irving and watched the girl athletes play tennis, Georgiana felt rested, inspired and optimistic. St. Louis was all in the past, and she intended to never think of it again.

The boat for Germany would sail in three months. Henry's copying machine was so useful, it must surely succeed. After a triumphant return to Chicago, his business would prosper, headquartered in one of the new downtown buildings, ten stories high. In a couple of years, three or four at the most, his copier would be found in offices all over Europe and America.

She saw herself decorating a large city apartment, overlooking the lake, where they would live for the first few years. Later, perhaps, when they needed more room, they could settle in a fine home up here. She would be an exemplary wife and mother, taking an active role in their church, serving on committees for the betterment of Society.

Doors would open.

— ⬩⬩⬩ —

FOR NOW, HOWEVER, she would spend the next three months, the last part of this whirlwind year, looking through windows. Train windows, hurtling to the next destination, and more hotel windows, watching and waiting for Henry to return from wherever he was.

She spotted him on the Philadelphia platform even before the train came to a stop, scanning the slowing windows for her face, and they waved to each other.

He was, as always, energetic, affectionate, bursting with plans.

"I've settled us in, we may be here for a month or more. There's some real interest in the copier. You'll like our landlady, you'll never believe it, but she's a licensed physician! Very admirable, we've had some excellent conversations." Her name was Mrs. Alcorn, though Henry, in private, jokingly called her Dr. Acorn.

Philadelphia was a good place to fall into her now familiar routine. She sought out a nearby Methodist church, a library, a teashop, a department store. These amenities were all in an easy walk, though the August weather sometimes kept her indoors. It may have been the heat, or something else, she couldn't say, but towards the end of the month, she suffered another, prolonged attack of her condition, the severest and longest one she ever had.

She refused to be seen when her eyes swelled up, though Henry insisted her fears were exaggerated, she didn't look bad at all. No matter, the debilitating headache and shakiness and heart palpitations were enough to keep her in bed, shades drawn. Dr. Alcorn stopped in often, pressing cool cloths on her forehead and urging her to eat.

Henry was in and out all though the month; sometimes he was gone a few days. Each time he returned, the news was better and better. Two bankers seemed ready to invest in the copier, the German partner started construction on the factory. He received a message from his lawyer that the title to the Fort Worth property was entirely cleared up. He was waiting for one more message, and then as soon as she felt well enough, they would go to Indianapolis.

"I can take care of several things there, and of course, we must see your family before we start overseas. And I would like your mother to store a few trunks for us."

"Won't we need them for the trip?"

"Certainly, some, but I think by the time we leave, we'll want to purchase some nicer, new ones," and he left her contemplating the pleasure of shopping in New York before the boat should depart.

The visitor he was waiting for stopped by on Saturday, the night of September 1st. Henry held his meeting in the parlor, and when he came back to the room, she was finally feeling better, sitting up in a chair.

"I need to be away tomorrow, to Nicetown," he said. "Are you able to start packing? I may want to be on the evening train."

She was about to object to travelling on the Sabbath, but stopped herself. She could still go to church in the morning, if she was up to it, and he seemed so keyed up tonight, really, barely able to contain himself. She didn't want hers to be a discouraging voice.

When Henry got back from Nicetown the following afternoon, he was out of breath, edgy and distracted.

"Good Lord, it's hot out there!" Henry wiped his face with a handkerchief that was already drenched. "Do you think it will be any cooler in Indiana?"

He went into the bathroom to rinse off and change, and handed her his damp clothing to pack when he was done.

"Let me rinse those out for you, I don't want to put them in like that," she said, kneeling over the nearly full trunk, but he shook his head.

"Sorry, but they won't have time to dry," and he hurried her along so they could make the late train, but just as they were about to leave, he stopped and sat her down in a chair with an air of great seriousness.

"I don't want to alarm you," he said, "but we may have a problem." He saw he succeeded in frightening her, and knelt down, pressing his hands on her knees.

"When I was out before, I saw a man I thought I recognized, hanging around outside. I could be wrong. But he looked like the Fort Worth man who set me up in St. Louis."

Georgiana put her hands on his.

"Just to be on the safe side, I'm going to tell Dr. Acorn we're going to Harrisburg. If they are following me, and they ask her where we've gone, she can send them in the wrong direction. I hope you don't think I'm being overly apprehensive?"

"Oh, no, Henry, you should do whatever you think is right. We've learned it's always better to err on the side of caution."

"In that case, let's do this. For the rest of the trip, when we sign into a hotel, I'm going to use a different name. There's no harm in it, it's not like we're skipping out on the bill. Is that all right with you?"

She gave him a sober nod, matching his intensity.

"Shall I record the different names in our book?"

He was momentarily confused, then his face cleared as he remembered the travel journal she was dutifully keeping.

"No," he said, "no, that's just for our own use. I think, though, the sooner you get to your mother's house, the better."

Henry was right. It was good to be home. He was solicitous, gracious, apologetic that he needed to leave on business right away, but would be back soon. He told Mary in confidence he was concerned for Georgiana's health. So much travel, though exciting, would take a toll on anyone, especially someone with an already overworked nervous system. Mary promised to look after her daughter with the care only a mother can provide, get her to eat more, and administer Henry's special medicine as often as needed. He squeezed her hand and thanked her profusely for taking care of the trunks.

When he returned, a few days later, Mary invited the Drakes for a meal, and afterwards, just as he had on his previous visit, Henry proposed a new and startling plan.

"I think we're all agreed," he said, with the air of a company president calling a meeting of the board of directors, "that Georgiana's welfare is the most important thing."

It was hard to argue with this sentiment.

"We'll be gone a long time, a far distance, across the ocean, and who knows what may happen? I want to take several steps to insure that, should anything ever happen to me, she, and Mary, and the boy, will be taken care of."

Georgiana's eyes misted at this.

"My Chicago property, which I own outright, is presently worth about $37,000."

The casual naming a figure so large almost caused Uncle Drake to drop his unlit pipe. Aunt Nan put a tight grip his free hand.

"I am deeding it to Georgiana, to be held in trust by Mary Yoke and William Drake, until we return."

The group was silent, awestruck, hanging on his every word.

"I want William," with a nod to Uncle Drake, "to execute a new mortgage on that property, in the amount of $10,000," and he had a ready answer to their worried frowns, brought on by the word "mortgage."

"The way to make money," he explained, "is to put your equity to work. The payments on the mortgage will be a minor expense for me. I'll arrange through my attorneys to have them made automatically. But the $10,000 will be at our disposal, to grow elsewhere. I like the prospects for Indianapolis right now. The recession has held prices down, it's very attractive for those with capital to invest."

William cleared his throat.

"I'm not sure, that is, am I the right one to do this? Nelson, after all, is her guardian. He's a city man, with more business experience than me," but Henry held up his hand, waving away such modesty.

"No," Henry said, "because he is the executor of the Yoke estate, and I want to invest Georgiana's share before we leave. Therefore, it would be a conflict of interest for him. No, the best man for the job is right here. I have all the instructions, no experience needed," and he extracted from his case a sheaf of papers, forms already filled out, and directions to the law firm of Leach & Barker to file the deed when it should arrive.

"Henry." Georgiana ventured one tremulous question. "That farm has been in our family for a long time. What do you mean by invest it? I shouldn't want to take any risk—"

Henry cut her short with another wave of the hand.

"Oh, my dear, no, it's simply making use of the equity while the estate is being settled. I daresay the portions of it won't be sold for quite a while, and meanwhile, should we let opportunity get away? No, sir! My plan is to use the capital against a nice little house. I have my eye on a few properties. We can make money renting it while we're gone, and when we return, either sell it at a profit, continue to rent it, or use it ourselves. Maybe," and now he turned to Mary, "maybe it's the sort of home you might like to live in sometime. Or if your boy is in school, or working in the city, just think how economical it would be for him to have a place already paid for! You can see the possibilities—"

Now Mary was caught up in the excitement.

"Why, that's a wonderful idea! Say, Henry," and here she hesitated, for she didn't want to interfere, but with so many tantalizing ideas before her, she plunged ahead.

"I own this house, outright, so I have equity too! Isn't that right? If you add in the deed to this house, I could be a partner. Then, I wouldn't feel as if we were imposing, if we did go to Indianapolis."

Henry immediately warmed to this idea, and gave his mother-in-law a broad smile.

"I could be persuaded," he said, and later, privately to Uncle Drake, he disclosed that he was prepared to add $750 to the deal. When he produced that amount, in cash, from an envelope in his case, Uncle Drake nearly fell out of his chair.

So it was that Georgiana and Henry spent a day in Indianapolis with Mr. Wright of the J. L. Wright Company, driving throughout the city, inspecting various houses. Mr. Wright understood that the exercise was purely for the wife's benefit. His brother, Worth Wright, who was also his partner, confided man to man that the client, the dapper looking Dr. Howard, already chose a house to purchase a few days earlier. The papers were all drawn up, and he had only to make the lady think the decision was hers. They chuckled over the subterfuge necessary when doing business with a woman, but didn't doubt the charming husband would persuade her to choose the right property.

But the Wrights weren't laughing when the deal collapsed.

"I'm sorry, Dr. Howard," said the earnest young man at the title company. "We must wait at least a week to execute this contract."

Georgiana was startled by Henry's face, angry and cold.

"The Yoke will states clearly, the lady must be twenty-five to exercise her portion of the estate. She is presently twenty-four."

"But she turns twenty-five next week! We're scheduled to leave town tonight. This is unacceptable."

"I can try to make an exception, if I have a certified letter from the executor of the estate. Why don't you visit him, and see what he says?"

"As her husband," Henry answered, "I'm responsible for her finances. I am over twenty-five, therefore, I can act for her."

"I regret," the young man said, "we would need a court ruling on that. The law of inheritance, as this office reads it, is clear. Why not just wait for a week? Then there is no issue."

"We could go see Uncle Nelson, Henry," Georgiana said. Her voice sounded timid to her own ears. "You need to call on him, anyway, before we leave. We keep missing him, every time we're in town."

Henry gave her a strangely blank look, as if he didn't hear what she said. He repeatedly bounced the bottom of his walking stick on the floor. It was quiet while Georgiana and the title man waited.

Then he smiled.

"That's a good idea. I'll stop over at the school, to make sure I catch him. You can go back to Franklin and finish packing," and without another word, he strode out of the office, leaving Georgiana to throw the man an apologetic little smile.

"Mrs. Howard!" called an unfamiliar voice, as she walked down Madison Street in Franklin. She was just finishing her errands, burdened with an armload of packages. As she turned towards the voice, one fell to the ground.

"Oh, I beg your pardon, let me get that for you," and she found herself thanking a rather nice looking young man she had never seen before.

"I am so sorry, I just wanted to give you my regards. I am acquainted with your uncle," the man said. "I'm from Chicago."

He never said which uncle, but since he was from Chicago, she assumed it was Uncle Isaac. He fell into step with her.

"I also have a passing acquaintance with your husband. I knew him in the city as Dr. Holmes," the young man said, "but now I hear he's called Dr. Howard."

"He changed his last name to meet the requirements of a family estate," she said.

"Ah, I see," he said, as though that happened every day.

Then he said, "He's quite an accomplished fellow. When did you meet him?"

"I went to Chicago for the World's Fair, found I liked the city, and determined to make it my home. Dr. Holmes was most helpful and kind to me there. We began to see each other, our friendship developed, and we were married in Denver last winter."

The young man nodded, and suddenly Georgiana started, wondering if she might be talking to a spy for the Fort Worth enemy.

"What did you say you do in Chicago?"

"Oh, I'm a reporter for the Tribune," he said, and showed her his card, then put it back in his pocket.

She felt relieved, and said goodbye. It never occurred to her to ask just what sort of story a Chicago reporter would be writing from Franklin, Indiana.

When she got home, Henry told her with great regret that once again, he was not able to meet Uncle Nelson, and now they really must hurry to catch their train.

She forgot to mention meeting his acquaintance, the reporter from Chicago.

"I'm awfully sorry we couldn't buy the house, Henry."

It was not rational to blame herself, of course. She couldn't help the date of her birthday, or the provisions of the will, but she felt guilty just the same.

They were back on the train, heading for Detroit.

"It's all right," he said, and then gave a long, sorrowful sigh. "It's just, well, there are some aspects, some thoughts I had about the use of the house, that I didn't share. I didn't want to upset you."

He moved from the seat across, to the empty one next to her, and put his hand over hers.

"I have to confess, you're a better judge of character than I am. You know that man, Mr. Lyman, the one you disliked so in Fort Worth?"

She nodded, wondering, what could that man have to do with them now?

"He's dead."

"Oh, that's too bad. What happened to him?"

"A dreadful accident, he was messing around with chemicals and had a lit pipe in his hand. The explosion took off half his face."

"Oh, my goodness, that's horrible."

"As you saw, he was consumed by drink. It probably happened while he was under the influence. Well, he left a wife, and a bunch of kids, I don't know, four or five, and the widow was too distraught to identify his body. The coroner's office found a letter from me among his possessions, and they asked me, when I was in Philadelphia, to do that unpleasant job for her."

"Philadelphia! What was he doing there?"

Henry shrugged. "He set up some sort of patent business. A last attempt, I guess, at some respectable endeavor. Anyway, when I performed that sad errand, I met the woman, and one of the daughters. Pathetic. I wanted to be helpful, so I considered, as an act of charity, letting her stay in the Indianapolis house for a while, until her affairs were settled."

"Oh, Henry! How kind of you. Now I'm doubly sorry it didn't work out," Georgiana said.

"Actually, I don't know if she would have accepted my offer. She's rather proud, because I did press some money on her, before I left, and she only took it with great reluctance."

Georgiana nodded. "I can understand that. When my father died, Mother had a lot of help from the family, though it always pained her to take it. But, she had me and Johnny to look after."

"A mother will do for her children what she will not do for herself," Henry pronounced. "However, what's past is past, so let's not talk about it any more. Let's think only of our future, which is looking brighter all the time."

Brightness was literally in her future. On October 17th, her twenty-fifth birthday, Henry presented a small box, and watched attentively as she lifted the lid, and gasped.

Inside rested a pair of earrings, magnificent dangling diamond earrings. They sparkled and winked at her when he held them up. She was stunned.

"Oh, the expense! Oh, my dear, how can you indulge me like this? What are you thinking?"

He smiled, for her response was just what he anticipated.

"You'll need some nice jewelry, and clothes to go with them, for the boat and for our travels in Europe. In fact, I've been thinking about that."

He reached for a pencil and blank pad, and scribbled a list on it.

"We'll get you some things here, in New York or Boston, but to make traveling easier I think we'll hold off on most of your wardrobe until we get to Europe. We might have some dresses ordered from Paris. My partner's son plays first violin for the symphony in Salzburg, we'll have to put in an appearance there, and there will be some dinners and receptions when the factory is finished. Also, if you pick up some fresh Paris designs just before we come back, you'll be a year ahead of anyone in Chicago. You'll need them, because by then you'll be in a position to join all the important women's clubs and charities, and I'm counting on you to expand our social circle."

He was uncanny, like a conjurer performing a trick. How had he guessed the things she privately imagined? And what man but Henry, besides Marshall Field himself, understood the annual cycle of women's fashions, from Paris to London to New York, then west from there to the rest of America?

He pulled out a batch of papers, and from among them took out a postcard without any writing on it.

"Look at this picture," he said. "My partner in Germany included this with his last letter."

A delicately tinted castle, a beautiful, ethereal structure, emerged straight up from the tip of a steep white mountaintop, as if sculpted by magic from the chalky stone. The black turrets of its several towers mimicked the peaks of a blue mountain range in the background. Green triangles of pine forest crept up to its base.

Along the bottom of the card, Gothic letters printed the words "*SCHLOSS NEUSCHWANSTEIN.*"

"They say the fellow who built it was insane," Henry said. "Mad King Ludwig, they called him. He bankrupted the countryside with projects like this, and everyone cursed him. Then he died, under mysterious circumstances, and the next week, they opened the castle up to tourists. Now, everyone makes money on it, and they bless his name!"

Georgiana laughed at this.

"I'm going to take you there," he said, and then he reached out his arms for her. She took another look before putting down the postcard.

"Well, I guess if you do, I'm going to need some new walking boots!"

He was watching her, with that now familiar, possessive look on his face.

"You know, Georgiana," he said, "for formal occasions, the women's gowns are cut low. Not overly modest. The line goes here," and he lightly traced his finger from her left shoulder to her right, dipping rather deeply in the middle. He led her to the bed, and reached underneath it for his medical bag.

She closed her eyes tightly and didn't make a sound when he sent a sharp needle into her tender earlobes, and before long, she was clad only in diamonds.

Now began a series of brief stops at various hotels in Detroit and Toronto. Henry's schedule was dictated by messages and telegrams that managed to reach him at all hours of the day or night. Occasionally they traveled apart. She could hardly keep up with where he was going at any one time, and once he surprised her by appearing on the same train she was on in mid-journey.

In these final heady days before they sailed, she seldom had time to establish the location of a church or other places to go, and so when she was alone, waiting for him to come back, she fell into the lazy habit of half dozing, half dreaming. Occasionally she took a small dose of Henry's patent medicine to forestall an attack of her condition. Sometimes she took a second dose. It left her pleasantly relaxed.

Once in a while, when she was bored, she held an earring up to a bright light, and marveled at the specks of quivering rainbows within each diamond, and lost herself then, in lovely reveries of what life would be like for them, so very soon.

A long table, covered by an immaculate white cloth, set with gold-rimmed, floral patterned china. Roses? Lilies? Gleaming utensils, real silver, not plate. Modulated voices, speaking well-educated sentences, punctuated by soft, agreeable laughter. She, seated next to Henry, draped in mauve? Or aqua? A gracefully low cut dress showing to best advantage her slender neck, her creamy shoulders that had never once been exposed to harsh sun. Her hair, elaborately styled up on her head in a pale gold crown. The diamond earrings sparkling, miniature versions of the dazzling crystal chandeliers casting a flattering light on the elegant party below.

Lake Forest? Prairie Avenue? London? Salzburg?

No, Germany. Her hostess would lean over and say, how clever your husband is, Mrs. Howard, he made such astute observations at the castle outing today. Is he an architect? Her nonchalant answer, oh no, he's trained as a physician, but has a great many interests, and designed a few buildings of his own back in the States.

Under a bright blue sky, in the fall, they would tour the Bavarian castle. She would hold Henry's arm as they ascended the steep steps up the mountain, hiking through a brilliant lower forest of crimson and copper. Wearing a new jaunty traveling suit, in beige or pearl gray? With a short jacket and slim skirt above the ankle, her hair tucked under a pert straw hat, she would navigate the terrain in new boots, wonderfully comfortable, of the softest leather. Italian, like the best ones carried by Siegel Cooper.

As Georgiana grew ever more languid and passive, Henry became ever more excitable. When did he sleep? She couldn't imagine, for as always he was gone before she woke up, and out most nights, only stopping in at midday to check on her and sort through his letters.

Abruptly, one day, he seemed to acknowledge his lack of attentiveness.

"I think we deserve a little bonus honeymoon trip," he announced. "I'm taking you to Niagara Falls."

"Really? Oh, Henry, I can't wait to send Mother a postcard from there!"

The postcard she sent implied they were there for a long trip, but actually it was only one day, which they thoroughly enjoyed together, but then Henry had to get back to Toronto for a meeting, then go to another town in Canada, then on to Vermont. He left her alone in Burlington for a few days – "too much travel, even for you!" — but when he returned he seemed finally satisfied, with a plan and a definite departure schedule.

"We'll make our way east, and sail from Boston, we'll probably be on the water by this time next week," he told her, and her heart jumped with excitement.

4

A COMPETENT WITNESS

November 1894 – November 1895

IT TURNED COLD in Boston by mid-November, and Georgiana wondered, on Saturday, if she should walk or take a cab to church the next day. Henry was busy checking the shipping offices for fares and departure dates. She window-shopped a little, but didn't mention the planned clothing purchases, because she noticed he seemed a little short of money. He hadn't complained about expenses, but the hotels they stayed in recently were definitely more economical than their accommodations had been at the beginning of the trip.

"I sent too much to my broker in Chicago," he finally explained, "I'll need him to wire some back. That's what you get for being too thrifty!"

She instantly felt guilty about the earrings, and he guessed her thoughts.

"It gives me comfort," he said, "to know that if anything should happen to me, you're taken care of. You should just think of the diamonds as one more security, like the Chicago property. Promise me you won't worry about them any more," and she breathed a deep sigh of relief, and gave her word.

So she was in a bright and hopeful state of mind when she heard a knock at the door early in the afternoon, expecting it was Henry, perhaps with an armful of packages, so he couldn't reach his room key. Instead, two men, one in uniform, the other in a plainclothes suit, stood in the hallway, official and grim.

"Mrs. Howard?" said the suited one. "I regret to tell you, your husband is under arrest. You are to surrender to us a diary, described by him as leather bound and written in your hand, which contains a record of your travels of this year."

The uniformed man held out a paper, presumably a warrant, which she brushed away.

"Arrested? What charge? You cannot be serious!"

The nightmare of St. Louis was repeating itself, but this time, she was less scared than angry. Could their enemy from Fort Worth really exert his evil influence this far?

"I cannot say. You will please wait here, do not leave town, until Superintendent Hanscom sends for you."

"I will not indeed! You are entirely mistaken. I will deliver the diary to him myself, and you will take me to my husband this hour!" She grabbed a coat and hat, put the book in her bag, and sailed out ahead of the men, who shrugged at each other and followed.

She spent the next several hours in a long hallway of the Boston police station, seated in a hard chair, watching officials hurry by, ignoring her. She was not allowed to see Henry.

A woman of about forty years, and a tall thin man about the same age, sat further down the hallway, whispering, occasionally interrupted by policemen with paper tablets, who asked questions, wrote quick notes, and strode away. At one point a policeman looked her way and pointed, and shortly after this, the woman rose and came to her, hand extended.

"Are you Herman's nurse?" she asked in a most friendly way.

Georgiana, lost in her own angry thoughts, assumed she was a mental case, and tried to ignore her.

"I'm Ellen, Herman's sister," the woman said, and pointed at the man. "That's our brother, Arthur Mudgett."

"I beg your pardon, you must have me confused with someone else," Georgiana said. Couldn't this foolish Ellen person see she had other things on her mind? Did she think this was a time and place to strike up some social acquaintance?

"Aren't you Miss Yoke?" Ellen asked. She was a plain woman, countrified, vague in manner, but her coloring and features were slightly familiar, like an older, plumper, female version of Henry.

"I'm the former Miss Yoke," Georgiana said, mystified. "My name is Mrs. Howard."

"Oh, our brother told us he changed his name to Howard. What a funny thing to do! He used to be Herman Mudgett. He told us all about you on his visit, how wonderful you were, to stay by his side and restore his health. Weren't we ever amazed to see him, after all this time! Was his operation terrible?"

"Operation?"

"To give back his memory, after the accident. Miraculous, what the doctors can achieve these days! Would you like to meet Arthur? Arthur, come here. Meet the pretty nurse who cared for Herman!"

The tall fellow shambled over.

"This is the lady Herman married after he lost his memory," Ellen said to him, and he held out his hand. Georgiana just looked at it.

"Arthur works here in Boston, so of course he came right over. Mother and Father can't leave the farm, but his wife Clara might come, and bring their boy to see him. Of course he told you all about them. Will you be returning to Denver, when the confusion about your marriage is all over, do you think?"

Georgiana was on the verge of coldly replying to this idiotic woman that no, there was no mistake, that Henry's previous marriage was invalid, and that the two of them were the victims of some elaborate joke, when they were interrupted by shouts at the end of corridor.

"Hold on, boys! Take it easy, we'll have something for you tomorrow," a large officer boomed, while two others held back a group of unruly men trying to push past, waving pads and pencils.

"Where's Carrie Pitezel? Are you charging her? Is Howard the same man as Holmes? Is that his wife?"

"Out, all of you! You'll get a statement tomorrow, I say!"

"Oh, dear," Ellen said, looking at Arthur.

He put his arm around her shoulders.

"We're not doing any good here. We've answered all their questions. Let's ask if we can leave now," he said, and he pulled Ellen away with a confused, backward look at Georgiana. Officers showed them to a side exit, and shortly afterwards, they led Georgiana to a small office where she could wait without being disturbed.

"What am I to think?" she stormed at Henry, an hour later, when she was finally allowed an audience with him. "What lies have been going on around here? Why didn't you tell me about these people? You told me your family were all dead!"

"They were dead to me!" he shouted back, the first time he ever raised his voice at her. Shocked, she folded her arms, and waited.

Henry sat back in his chair, and studied her, taking his time. He showed not the slightest nervousness about the fact that they were arguing in a jail cell, nor did he seem worried about the angry and baffled wife before him.

"I suppose," he said, "as a teacher, you are taught to feel sorry for the slowest children in the class, the dolts. You give them extra help, so they can keep up with their brighter peers, so they don't have to suffer shame, isn't that right?"

She nodded, wondering what that had to do with anything.

"Did you ever consider, then, the agony, the torture, how it feels to be the smartest, most clever child, in the class, in the town, in the whole county? Can you imagine what it was like, for me, to grow up among such idiots? You saw Ellen. Did you not notice the look of sheer stupidity on her face? Her passing resemblance to a cow?"

"Henry," she protested. He leaned forward, hands clenched in tight fists on his lap.

"From my earliest days, I could run circles around those two. A decade older than I was, and I could beat them at anything. I could read before I was three. I read every book in the county before I was out of short pants. I knew the answer to every problem before half the words were out of the teacher's mouth! When I was nine, *nine*, Georgiana, I could make up a speech right off the top of my head, and convince them I was quoting Lincoln!

"It became a game for me, to relieve the unrelenting boredom of my life, my only entertainment, really, to invent stories, the more preposterous the better, and test how gullible were the people all around me. Stupid, stupid people! My parents, my brother and sister, neighbors, classmates, what right did any of them have, to be in charge of anything, to be in charge of *me*, when they were all so impossibly stupid?

"Do you want to know what my father said, when I told him I wanted to go to college? Do you? He said, stay here, be a farmer, don't get above yourself! Can you imagine? I, not go to college? Fool old man.

"So, when I saw them again, I just fell back into that old habit, just for the fun of it. I made up a whopper, all about you. Of course, I never thought they would repeat my tall tale to anyone else! That's a rather fitting revenge for them, I suppose."

"Why didn't you tell me you were going to see them?"

"I thought about it. I considered taking you to meet them, but first I wanted to see if time, and maturity, had eased my hostility, my anger, and my shame of them."

Georgiana took off her glove and rubbed her head.

"And what about this woman Clara? I remember you told me she was dead."

"I said I *heard* she was, I wasn't sure. But it doesn't matter. The marriage was annulled, as I told you."

"*She* doesn't seem to think so! Ellen said she was coming, and bringing a boy with her. Your boy!"

"Ellen wasn't even living at home when all that happened, so what does she know? Clara might be looking for some excuse for the existence of that boy, but he isn't mine. And Georgiana, just consider this. I haven't been back there for years. If she thought we were still married, why didn't she sue for abandonment? If I left her with a child, why didn't her father come after me? I had Christmas cards from people in Gilmanton, for Heaven's sake, they knew where I was! They could have found me, if any reason to existed!"

His plausibility wore her down.

"Well, all right then. So what is this all about? What in the world are they holding you for? I heard such strange things while I was waiting out there! Who is this woman they keep talking about, this Carrie Pitezel person?"

Now Henry shifted to sadness.

"I did mislead you on a certain point, Georgiana. I'm sorry. The man who came to see me, that night in Philadelphia, it wasn't about the copier. It was Ben Pitezel, the man you knew in Fort Worth who went under the name of Lyman."

"The dead man? The one who drank?"

"Yes, that's the one. I did some business dealings with him, more than I led you to believe, and some of them, I'm sorry to say, were on the sharp side, perhaps not strictly legal.

"The Fort Worth squatter is still out to make trouble for me. He got hold of some information about Pitezel, and his wife. That's the woman they spoke of, she's been charged with fraud. They planned an insurance fraud together, and the lawyer, Mr. Howe, was apparently also involved."

"The lawyer! The one that got you out in St. Louis! That's awful, Henry," she said.

"Well, it makes it look rather bad on my part. I may have to postpone our trip. I'm so sorry," Henry said, with a hint of tears in his eyes.

"What happens now?"

They managed to keep her family from hearing of the St. Louis debacle. Could they possibly suppress this latest humiliation?

"I think the police are taking me back to Philadelphia. It seems they want to ask me some questions there."

The nighttime train journey to Philadelphia was uncomfortably chilly and impossibly strange.

Georgiana sat alone in the back of the car, silent, stiffly refusing any offers of food or water. Midway up was the woman, Mrs. Pitezel, with a girl in her teens and a baby they handed back and forth. The baby cried every so often, setting Georgiana on edge and unreasonably adding to her fury.

The woman didn't look anything like the crafty female criminal Georgiana imagined her to be. She looked instead as if, rather than sitting on the train, it had rolled right over her. She was haggard and strained, her pallor evident even in the dim nightlight. An officer sat next to her, awkward and even more put off by the baby than Georgiana was.

Some men from the defrauded insurance company were there too, not that anyone bothered to introduce himself or explain a single thing to her. Then up front, just out of earshot, handcuffed to another officer, was Henry, inexplicably cheerful, even exuberant. She couldn't hear what he was saying, but every so often a guffaw or bit of laughter reached her, and the sound of it made her angriest of all.

When they arrived at last, the two prisoners were led away for interrogation. Mrs. Pitezel cried out when a matron took the young girl and the baby away. The insurance men departed with some police detectives, presumably to find an open tavern, and she was left sitting, ignored once again, until finally some assistant from the district attorney's office said she could go. He hailed a cab outside to take her to a nearby hotel.

"You're not charged with anything," the assistant said, "but we will want to interview you soon. Don't leave town, and if I were you, I'd avoid talking to any reporters."

Two days later, Georgiana was summoned to the office of District Attorney George Graham.

Clerks bearing reams of documents scurried past bulging half open file drawers. There were no girl typists here, only men, intent and mechanical behind their machines.

An officer led her to a separate conference room in the back of the office, a plain space with just a few chairs around a long table, where Mr. Graham and his assistant, Mr. Barlow sat, along with two clerks, busy with notepads and pencils.

Mr. Barlow held a photograph out, and said, "Miss Yoke, do you know who this is?"

She didn't look at the photograph.

"Please call me Mrs. Howard, for that is my name," Georgiana said, with ice in her voice.

"I apologize," he said, with a glance over at Mr. Graham. "Mrs. Howard, please tell us what you know of the woman in the picture."

Georgiana looked, expecting to see an image of Carrie Pitezel.

"Why, that's Miss Williams, a secretary employed by my husband. I only ever saw her once."

"Was it recently that you saw her?"

"No," Georgiana said. "She was to ride on the train with us to Denver last January, but changed her mind at the last minute. I can tell you, Henry was most put out about it, because he counted on getting some dictation finished on the train, and having letters typed on our arrival. I have no skill at such work, even if he would let me, and so he had to hire some secretarial service when we got there."

"What reason was given for her change of plan?"

Graham leaned forward, and the clerk's pencils hovered over their notepads.

"Some romance, Henry said. She was a flighty, thoughtless girl. Why do you wish to know about her?"

Barlow ignored her question, and followed with another one.

"Has your husband corresponded with her? Received any letters you know of, since then? During your travels this last year, perhaps?"

"No, I'm sure not. That is, he has a great deal of correspondence, but he never mentioned any. I'm sure he would have said, 'Oh fine, *now* she writes!' if a letter ever came from her."

"Why was she going to Denver?"

"She had some family there, and was going to visit them. A few of the girls from the office at first were planning to go on a lark, as Henry was closing the office for the year and they had no work to do, but then the rest of them got other jobs, and it was just Miss Williams left. Perhaps traveling with her employer and his wife was not as amusing a prospect as it seemed when her friends were going to be along."

There was silence in the conference room for a while, as the men digested this intelligence. Mr. Barlow next brought out a set of three photographs, of a boy and two girls, and laid them on the desk.

"Have you ever seen these children before?"

Georgiana shook her head.

"Never."

"They are the children of the dead man, Ben Pitezel," Mr. Barlow said, "and they've gone missing."

"I never saw them before in the whole of my life. I never heard the name, until Boston. I'm sorry, and I'm sorry for the mother, but I cannot help you."

"Your husband told us the children are with Miss Williams, and that he paid her to take them to London. What do you think of that?"

Corruption. Bribery. The dishonest, cutthroat world of men, just as Henry said.

"I think that is a monstrous lie, and it was invented by you." She looked right at Mr. Graham. "I think that my husband has powerful enemies, that the police are paid by them, and that this conspiracy will not succeed in the end."

She folded her arms, defiant.

"He warned me about you," she added.

"*He* warned you about *us!*" Graham pointed his pencil at her. "That's pretty rich. Young woman, your man is a swindler, a liar, and very possibly a killer. You are placed in a precarious spot indeed, and the sooner you get past your delusions about him, the better off you'll be," but he broke off, for it was obvious he wasn't getting through to her. He gestured to the clerks to take her out.

A note arrived at her hotel from Henry's lawyer, saying she would not be allowed to visit for the time being, but that he was in good spirits, and hoped matters would be cleared up soon. She should answer any questions the police had for her as briefly as possible, and speak to no one else, and ignore any wild rumors being printed in the newspapers.

They brought her back the following week. Again, District Attorney Graham sat silently at the end of the long table, and again Mr. Barlow started the questions, more careful this time in his approach.

"Perhaps someone would bring in the certificates?" he said, and a clerk left the room.

"There seems to be some dispute about your name, ma'am. I wonder, if there is a chance we might be friends, for I've no wish to be your enemy, if I might sidestep the issue and call you Miss Georgiana?"

It was not fine at all, but she didn't say anything.

"We are working on several mysteries at the same time. The first is the matter of the insurance fraud, in which your husband has confessed to a role. The second is the strange circumstances of the death of Mr. Pitezel. The third is the supposed connection of the Pitezel children to the typist, Miss Williams. But our most important mission is to find those missing children. You must understand, as a woman, how frantic their mother is! The sooner they are found, the sooner your husband is not suspected in their disappearance. It is utterly in your own interest to help us, you know. You must see that," and he smiled, in such a sympathetic way, her anger faded despite her best efforts to keep it stoked.

"I'm very sorry for that woman," Georgiana replied. "I saw on the train from Boston how ill she looked, but I really cannot help you."

"Did you not have a calendar, or diary, of your journey?"

"Yes, but I gave it to the police, and they took all the information they wanted from it."

"We may need to see it again," Barlow said. "More evidence has come to light since then," but stopped when the clerk returned with a packet. He took two documents from it and placed them face down on the table.

"You've probably seen in the papers, and you met his family, so you now know your husband's name is really Herman Webster Mudgett. He changed it, first to Holmes, and then to Howard. Can you tell us why he changed his name the first time?"

"He didn't much like his family, they were estranged, so I guess he just wanted a different name from them. Then when his uncle died, he took his name, to inherit some property." She added defensively, "Lots of people change their names. If you look in the back of any newspaper, you can see them listed."

Barlow turned over the documents.

"I'm going to show you two certificates of marriage. The first, dated 1878, shows Herman Mudgett, united in marriage to Clara Lovering, in Alton, New Hampshire. The second, dated 1887, shows the marriage of H. H. Holmes to Myrta Belknap in Cook County, Illinois. There has been no divorce recorded in either case, and both women are living. Now do you understand why I invoked your maiden name?"

Georgiana's cheeks flamed, but she kept her composure.

"It was an honest mistake on your part, I'm sure. I'm aware of these two people, but the situation is not as you suppose. The first, the one in New Hampshire, you can see by the date took place when Henry was young, just eighteen. It was merely a childhood fancy, within a week they both knew it was a mistake, and the girl's father paid someone in court and had it annulled immediately. I suppose you didn't look for a document of annulment?"

One of the clerks ducked his head, and from their pained looks she could tell she was right. She continued, her voice stronger now.

"As to the second, well, Henry told me all about that. The woman is an adventuress, who imposed herself on my husband when he was new to Chicago. As soon as he achieved some financial success, she disclosed that she was having a child."

Every man in the room looked embarrassed.

"He is a medical man, as you know, and he understands all about these things. He calculated the child could not be his own, but he is such a gentleman, with such scruples, that he chose to support it anyway, and set them up in a household north of Chicago, in Wilmette. Of course, he could not marry her, knowing there were other men in her life.

"This document is a fake, and that woman is perfectly capable of perpetrating such a fraud. She is also a fanatic, and mentally unstable, in her belief that she retains some hold on him. It really is rather sad and pathetic," and Georgiana drew a deep breath, and was done.

The men remained silent, stunned, until at last Graham pushed back his chair.

"The man is brilliant! He's a genius!"

Georgiana stared angrily at him, and he stared right back at her.

"I mean it, I salute him! I take my hat off to him! Who else could possibly invent such a pile of rubbish?"

He stood.

"The normal rules of decency don't apply to him, oh no! He abandons one wife, and a son. He fakes marriage to the mother of his love child, and just see who defends him!"

His fist slammed the table.

"The stage has missed the greatest actor of our century! I only thank God he never went into police work," and he stomped out of the room, followed by the clerks, leaving Georgiana and Barlow alone, to face one another across the table.

The silence was long and awkward, finally broken by Barlow.

"Loyalty in a wife is a wonderful thing, Miss Georgiana," he said softly, and she felt warmth behind her eyes, and prayed the tears would not fully form and spill out.

"We're not so bad as you've been led to believe, you know," he went on, "though no doubt some police are corrupt, most of us just want to catch criminals. We have no interest in pursuing an inno-cent man. We're plenty busy with all the guilty ones on the loose! I like to think Philadelphia is a bit safer for our efforts."

He smiled at her, kindly and with pity, and she felt herself relenting, despite being profoundly insulted by his boss. He pulled out a handkerchief, but she shook her head, so he put it away again.

Outside the conference room, District Attorney Graham regained his temper, though not any degree of cheer, when he regarded the door after Georgiana was escorted out.

"Heaven help us if our evidence rests on her."

"It won't come to that, sir, there's the medical, and so much else," Barlow said, but Graham shook his head.

"It all depends on what the judge will allow, and it's just such a damn *strange* case!"

He leafed through a file.

One of the clerks, a new one, without much experience, said, "I'll bet, with all the charges waiting for him in Fort Worth, and St. Louis, he'll get taken down one way or another."

It was the wrong thing to say.

The other clerks fixed their eyes on their papers, and held their breath, waiting for an explosion. Barlow rolled his eyes. The District Attorney turned his gaze on the unfortunate youth, and enunciated very clearly.

"It will *never* be said that this office was the one to let H. H. Holmes slip away. If he's done even half of what I suspect he has, we'll try him, we'll convict him and *we* will make him hang. Let no one in here ever forget it!"

———— ∞ ————

THE GRUESOME DEATH of insurance swindler Benjamin Pitezel in Philadelphia, and the arrest of his wife and accomplice in Boston, was widely reported in the major newspapers. Interest turned to excitement when Mrs. Carrie Pitezel confessed to her part in the scheme, implicating both the lawyer Jeptha Howe and the master-mind Dr. Howard, known to her as Dr. H. H. Holmes.

A jubilant pack of Chicago reporters sprinted from their offices on Calhoun Place, pushed through the heavy oak door of Henry Koster's private newsman's club, tossed their bowlers in the general direction of a hat rack, and slung themselves into their usual chairs.

"Open a fresh barrel of Berghoff, Henry! It's going to be a long night!"

Matches struck, lighting pipes, cigars and cigarettes. Glasses were filled, feet set up on tables, and serious drinking commenced.

"I've been on the trail of that Holmes bastard for years," said a young Tribune man. "Can't believe they finally caught up to him. Cheers, to Philadelphia!"

Through the effusive haze, a newcomer said, "So who is this fellow? What's he done?"

All attention turned to the Tribune.

"I have a list as long as my arm, but here's something, just to get the flavor of the man. A couple years ago I interviewed a fellow, head of a gang of carpenters, who worked on this monstrosity of a building for Holmes, commonly known as the Castle. At the end of the week, he goes to collect their wages, and what do you think? He not only refuses to pay, but says they're all fired for shoddy work. My fellow protests, says they followed the building plan exactly, but Holmes just gives him a murderous look and dares him to contest the claim."

"Bastard all right! So what happened? Did they make a complaint?"

"They did, but of course nothing came of it. Who cares about working men?"

"Our gendarmes are too busy, fighting crime over at the Everleigh House!"

Glasses clinked.

"But here's the really strange part. A little while later, the very same thing happened to another fellow. Then *he* put me on to *another* one! Same story, the same cheat. This went on for a year, until the place was finished."

"So the whole place was built on free labor? There's a nimble trick!"

"And it was all his own plan, never had a professional architect. But my friend said it was the queerest building he ever saw. His crew put in a hallway with no doors. It led to nowhere."

"Not the talent he thought he was! So what happened in Philadelphia?"

The Tribune man wiped beer foam from his mustache with his sleeve.

"There was a scheme, between Holmes, this man Ben Pitezel, and Pitezel's wife. They take out a big life insurance policy on Ben, find some other man's dead body, stage an accident to disfigure the face so no one can say it isn't him, and identify it as Ben. The widow makes the claim, and the three split the proceeds. Clear so far?"

"Audacious. Inspired," the younger man said, taking a deep swill from his stein. "I love it. I want it. Where's my typewriter?"

"This one's mine, already filed, sorry. But hold on. It gets better," the reporter said. "My pal in Philadelphia got the whole story from his brother in the coroner's office. They can't prove it yet, but their theory is Holmes duped his own partners. He chloroformed Pitezel, and then he set the explosion that took off his face. There never was any substitute body."

Silence all around, as these cynical men, who thought they had heard everything, considered the viciousness of the plot, and its author.

Finally a reporter from the Inter-Ocean spoke.

"You say he blew up the man's face?"

"So it couldn't be recognized."

"Sweet Jesus," the man said. "I only wonder, when he set off the explosion, was Pitezel already dead, or was he still alive?"

George and Nelson Yoke took the evening train to Franklin as soon as they got Mary's frantic message. Reporters had camped outside her house, had knocked on the door throughout the day, wanting to know everything she could tell them about Henry, about Georgiana, about Minnie Williams, about the missing children of some woman named Carrie Pitezel.

"I got a postcard from Toronto, she was fine!" Mary cried. "They went to Niagara Falls, everything was fine. They were getting ready to sail. Why doesn't she ever tell me anything!"

"Now, Mary, we don't know all the facts," Nelson said. "Maybe there's some confusion, Howard is a common last name, after all, we don't know it's even the same man," but she shook her head.

"The newspaper men knew all about him, that his name used to be Holmes, in Chicago, all about his building there. No, it's the same one. He must be a scamp! I only pray he doesn't have Georgiana implicated in some scheme," but what exactly was happening remained a mystery to the family because, as days became weeks, and despite urgent telegrams and letters to Philadelphia, Georgiana refused to come home. A terse note back from her contained only the barest consolation.

"I must stay here until this situation is cleared up. Henry's lawyer is advising me. Please don't worry, and don't talk about it to anyone outside the family."

IT WAS CHRISTMASTIME in Philadelphia, dreary, cold and depressing. Since that terrible day of Henry's arrest in November, she kept to herself, hiding out in the hotel, talking only to Henry's attorney or the police when summoned, not even venturing out to church, for fear of reporters. She had been allowed only two brief, closely supervised visits since then.

A letter from Henry arrived on his lawyer's stationery.

"Will you do something for me? I need you to go to Chicago. There are some papers in my safe, in the Englewood building, that will help my case. I can't trust anyone else. If the police get a hold of them, if they even know about them, they'll be destroyed."

He added, *"My dearest Georgiana, I've been in prison every day of my life, except for the days I had with you."*

────※────

WHERE TO STAY in Chicago?

Here was a dilemma. Uncle Isaac's business had taken him permanently to Ohio, and now someone else occupied the apartment on State Street. She fretted that she might run into someone from the store, someone who would have read about Henry in the papers, but then again, it was a big city. She settled on the Saratoga, a large hotel on Dearborn Street.

She sent a message to Mary Ellen, telling herself with some self-pity she might be her only remaining friend. They met at the restaurant of the hotel, and took a streetcar south to the sprawling Englewood building. It looked run down, quiet, still in disrepair from the upper level fire.

"I'll wait outside," Mary Ellen said, although it was bone cold.

"I don't know how long it will take," Georgiana said, so Mary Ellen walked down the street to a shop, and Georgiana went in alone.

Pat Quinlan, Henry's caretaker, took the sealed letter Henry sent, and read his instructions.

"Henry forgot the combination," Georgiana said. "He told me to bring everything," and she opened the top of an empty briefcase.

It didn't take long to fill it with the jumble of papers from the safe. She looked around the empty office while Mr. Quinlan finished, and then he walked her out. They saw Mrs. Quinlan on the way, and they were introduced, but Mrs. Quinlan didn't seem to want to talk.

They stood on the curb for a little while, waiting for Mary Ellen, and Georgiana finally said, "I just don't know anything anymore!

He says one thing, and I believe it, and then another thing happens, and it can't be true. What do you think, Mr. Quinlan, is there any end in sight to this business?"

He gave her a sly look.

"What troubles he has, he's brought on himself. There's nothing you can do."

"Maybe," Georgiana said, "I should pay a visit out to Wilmette, and at least set matters straight there."

Quinlan laughed. "You'd better have some protection if you do, or that woman will tear your eyes out!"

"That confirms what I thought, she must be crazy," Georgiana said. When Mary Ellen rejoined her, she could see Georgiana was upset, but was too polite to press for details.

It was only at lunch, back at the Saratoga, Georgiana confided, nothing about Henry, but her reluctance to visit home in Franklin, for fear of gossip and people turning up their noses at her.

"They never liked me there!" she said. "I wish Mother never left Edinburgh," and Mary Ellen nodded in sympathy.

"You know how people in a little country town can be," she said.

"I will never, ever live there again, no matter what else happens," Georgiana vowed, but she spoke too soon.

When she brought the papers to Mr. Shoemaker, he asked her to stop in his office. He shut the door.

"It's a miracle you got back here with these. I think you may have been followed in Chicago."

"What? You mean by the Fort Worth squatters?"

"No, by the police. Shortly after you left, Mr. and Mrs. Quinlan got a pretty unpleasant visit. I'm sure they had to say you were there."

He pulled out a chair for her, and sat opposite.

"Mrs. Quinlan was put in the sweatbox, apparently told to confess to all sorts of ridiculous things."

"That poor woman! Henry tried to tell me about things like that, how cruel and dishonest the police can be, but I never believed such things were possible."

"Under that kind of pressure, people will say anything," he agreed. Then he said, "Mrs. Howard, have you been in touch with your mother lately?"

"Well, we've written, but this would hardly be a pleasant time to pay a visit at home."

"Police detectives and reporters have been questioning her," he said. "There's a search going on for your husband's former secretary, Minnie Williams. Your mother told all of them that Minnie Williams went to Denver with you, that she witnessed your wedding. This doesn't square at all with your husband's story. Can you tell me why your mother said this?"

Georgiana felt her face redden.

"When we traveled out to Denver, Miss Williams was supposed to go, but at the last minute she changed her mind. So we didn't have anyone we knew to chaperone. Afterwards, it didn't seem worthwhile to mention it to Mother, it would only have upset her."

"Why didn't he just say so? Why does he have to make up these elaborate charades? It's as if he's just baiting the police!"

"That may well be, Mr. Shoemaker. He has contempt for people he thinks are stupid. It's a terrible failing of his."

Shoemaker sighed.

"I'm going to advise him to plead guilty to the fraud charges."

"If he is guilty of fraud, then he should plead guilty," Georgiana said.

"That's very stoic of you, Mrs. Howard. Some women wouldn't stick by their husband in a situation like this."

"I don't believe in divorce, if that's what you're suggesting," Georgiana said. "I believe anyone can be redeemed. Henry is too ambitious. He was carried away by greed. I know that now. He lied to me about his family, and lied to them about me, and that was a wrong thing to do. But I can still forgive him, if he is truly repentant. It's just so hard, with all these mad stories and rumors about him. I don't feel like I can speak to anyone right now."

"It must be hard for you. Of course, his enemy from Fort Worth has caused all this trouble, and the newspapers love it. Pay no attention."

"I won't, I promise. I don't even look at them."

"Wouldn't the police just love to have a scapegoat for all their unsolved cases, to make themselves look good! But in the end, it will only come down to what they can prove."

"What does that mean?"

"I expect him to get two years," Shoemaker said. "He seems resigned to it. There is nothing you can do to help him now, but go back home. Go home and see your family. And keep your mother away from reporters!"

———

IT WAS HUMILIATING to be living back at home. The goodness of her family only made it worse.

Mary was kind, solicitous. Her hands fluttered, jittery and nervous, as she prepared special food, tried to get Georgiana to take the good bed, carefully avoided saying anything about Henry. Her fingers constantly twisted the edge of a handkerchief tucked into her sleeve, a gesture Georgiana found particularly annoying.

Uncle Nelson sent a welcoming, generous letter, promising a visit as soon as the school year was finished, without a single reproachful word. Johnny didn't even smirk, just grunted hello and said she could have his room when school was out, as he was planning to help Uncle George at the farm all summer.

She had been home for several weeks when she came into the kitchen one afternoon and found her mother deep in conversation with a burly, heavily mustached man, drinking tea at her kitchen table.

"This is Mr. Geyer," Mary said, as if introducing an old friend.

The man stood, and gave a slight, somber bow. He identified himself as a detective, hired out by the defrauded insurance company to assist the police. It was as before in Philadelphia, all about the missing children.

"I wish I could help you," she said, for the hundredth time. "I never saw them, I have no idea where they are."

Mary gave Georgiana her seat and left them alone.

"I know, and I believe you. I really want to talk about Henry. I think your husband is an extraordinary man. I've been thinking a lot about him, these past few weeks, trying to figure this thing out. There is a great deal, you know, in this case, that doesn't make any sense.

"I wonder if you can think of anything, some thing about him, that might account for this situation. You must admit, his way of life is unusual, to say the least. Most folks don't travel, or conduct business, in such an *intense* manner, if you see what I mean. Can you just help me understand him a little better?"

She thought about it for a moment.

"He's a man who might work until three o'clock in the morning, and never notice he's tired. Then, he might lock the door of his shop and go for a bicycle ride at two in the afternoon! He makes his own rules for living.

"He can learn anything, master any subject he sets his mind to, medicine, architecture, anything, with almost no effort. He is completely confident in his abilities. Perhaps that is a failing. It's possible his sharp business practices crossed the line of the law, and so he has enemies. He is ambitious, overly so, but what man of genius is not?"

"Men of genius are often selfish," he noted. "I have to wonder, in all these travels last year, did he ever consider your wishes? And did you really feel you could trust him?"

She looked at his surprisingly gentle expression, and although they could not have been more dissimilar, something about him reminded her of Uncle Nelson. The thought unexpectedly popped into her mind, *this man has known loss.*

"Yes," she said. "Yes, once I made up my mind to marry him, I did not entertain any doubts."

"What would it take to convince you to testify for the prosecution?" Geyer asked. "What if we found the children, dead, murdered, and could prove that he had a hand in it? Would you cross over then?"

Georgiana shook her head, and gave him a pitying look.

"Your difficulty is, the things you are trying to accuse him of are the acts of a madman, and Henry is perfectly sane, just as sane as you are. Maybe he broke the law, because he was impatient to get rich. Maybe he tells lies. But no one would just murder children, why would they? Those children most likely ran away, because they had a drunkard for a father and a swindler for a mother. It's sad, but they're probably in the hands of criminals who take up street children. That is the most likely explanation, and in all your years of experience, you know the most likely solution is what eventually is proved true."

"You may be right, and I hope and pray you are," Mr. Geyer said. "But I think you are mistaken. He need not be insane, but I think Henry led a secret life, one he was able to keep from you, and during those times, he did terrible things. I don't know why. But if we can prove he is connected to the children's deaths, will you help us?"

She smiled at the preposterousness of his challenge.

"Very well. If you find them murdered, Heaven forbid, and prove he was involved, I'll testify for you," and he extended a hand to make her shake on the bargain.

MISSING GIRLS' BODIES FOUND IN TORONTO

Toronto, Ont. -- July 16, 1895. The bodies of Alice Pitezel, aged 15, and Nellie Pitezel, aged 11, missing daughters of Benjamin Pitezel, were discovered buried under a cellar on Vincent Street. The police believe the girls were suffocated with gas by H. H. Holmes, the man suspected of killing their father in Philadelphia. A third child, Howard, aged 8, is still missing, and is thought to have been similarly murdered in another city by Holmes, the desire being to rid himself of three beings who might rise to convict him of the other crime.

Detective Geyer of Philadelphia has been for several days in this city searching for traces of the girls who disappeared last October while in the charge of Holmes. The owner of the Vincent Street house identified a photograph of Holmes as the man who rented the house at the time in question.

Bright morning sun through the kitchen window warmed the white pages blazing the stark black headline. She stared at the words, then at her terrified face in the mirror.

"No, this can't be true, this must be a dream, a terrible dream, I need to wake up," she told herself, and to prove it really was a dream, she smashed the mirror, fully expecting to snap into wakefulness before it hit the floor.

Mary came running at the noise, and found Georgiana kneeling among shattered pieces of glass, tearfully picking them up and apologizing and rambling about seven years of bad luck.

Later that morning, two telegrams arrived.

The first, as expected, was from the District Attorney's office in Philadelphia.

"Justice requires your return to Philadelphia. Notify office when arriving, an escort will meet train. Keep receipts for reimbursement of travel expenses. Avoid speaking to press."

The other one was from Henry's lawyer.

"Do not despair. No proof connects Henry with Toronto discoveries. We believe arrest of real culprit imminent. He sends love, misses you, urge you stay in Franklin. Say nothing to reporters."

Holding a telegram in each hand, she imagined two men.

Henry's probing blue eyes, fixed on hers, coming up with new excuses.

Mr. Geyer's steady gaze, darkened by sorrow, pleading for her help.

Henry's fingertip touch.

Mr. Geyer's honest handshake.

Her marriage vow.

Her promise to the law.

Watching her daughter from the kitchen doorway, Mary said, "What are you going to do?"

Georgiana laid the telegrams on the table, tearless now, grim and resolute.

"I have to start packing."

The next day, Mary was straining to lift the heavy iron down from the shelf above the stove, getting it ready to heat for the laundry Georgiana was pulling off the line. From the front room, she heard a quick hard knock, followed by a man's voice calling, "Hello, Mrs. Yoke? Mrs. Howard? Anybody here? Just a couple of questions, if you please."

By the time she set the iron on the stove and untied her apron, two reporters were already roaming inside the house, studying Georgiana's portrait and copying down the titles on Mary's bookshelf.

"Oh, terribly sorry," said one, with no actual apology in his voice. "We weren't sure if you could hear us."

The other held a pencil over his notepad.

"We understand the District Attorney has summoned Mrs. Howard, can you confirm, is she going to Philadelphia?" Before Mary could compose an answer, the quarry herself appeared, bringing in a basket full of clothes.

Georgiana was horrified to find her mother, flustered and intimidated by the two strangers, and further, to realize that both of her telegrams still lay in plain sight on the table. She quickly set the basket down on top of them.

An open, half-packed trunk by the bedroom door gave the answer to the first question, so they fired the next one.

"What can you tell us about the Pitezel children, Mrs. Howard?"

She thought of the warnings in the telegrams, and swallowed hard.

"Upon that subject I have nothing to say."

"We have a report you will swear Holmes was not in Toronto at the time the Pitezel children were murdered. Can you confirm that?"

"I decline to make any statement on that subject," Georgiana said, in the hope that with no cooperation they would leave her alone, but Mary now found her voice.

"Why, that report is certainly not true!"

Georgiana prayed her mother wouldn't offer to show them her postcard from Niagara Falls. For the first time, it occurred to her how impossible her position was, how guilty she must seem. She would have to say something in her own defense.

"But you admit you were in Indianapolis last fall, when Holmes had custody of the children? Did you know them? Did you know they disappeared?"

She sat down, straight-backed, and folded her hands in her lap.

"Why, I never knew there was such a family in existence. How could I know what became of the boy? I never heard of the Pitezel family until my husband was arrested."

"But you knew the father of the children? Ben Pitezel?"

"Yes, but he went under another name in Fort Worth. I never knew he had a family."

Now came a new, unexpected line of attack.

"What do you know about Holmes' other wives?"

All Henry's explanations, so reasonable-sounding in Chicago and Boston, now seemed absurd. Was there any way these inquisitors would believe she was anything but a fool or a criminal? Excruciatingly, in front of her mother, she had to come up with some excuse for herself.

"I know nothing about that, I mean, I heard it said, but —"
Mary interrupted.

"There is no reason to think Mr. Howard ever married any other woman than my daughter. They were married in January, in Denver, and I have the marriage certificate right here in my possession, and it's perfectly proper."

"Where did you live after Denver, Mrs. Howard?"

"We were in Fort Worth, from February through April, and after that, well, just about everywhere."

"And in all that time, you really didn't think there was anything wrong? Any suspicions about his business?"

She saw a judgment in the eyes of one of the men, as certain as any medieval witch-dunker.

"No," she said. They waited, but she added nothing to her answer, other than, "Please, leave us alone now, and let me finish my packing."

The reporters made their way through the cornstalk path, and one paused at the corner to light a cigarette.

"What do you think?" the reporter with the notepad said.

"Guilty as sin," said the other, shaking out his matchstick. "She's up to her pretty little neck in it, the swindles, maybe even the murders. How could she not be?"

"Georg-i-ana from In-di-ana," the first one chanted. "Oh, she's in a real pickle, all right. But I don't think she went along with him. Seems too upright to me."

"Well, you can write it your way, I'll write it mine. We'll give the old man both, and see which way he wants to play it." He looked towards the business district of Franklin. "Do you suppose there's a telephone anywhere in this town?"

AFTER THE DISCOVERY of the dead Pitezel girls in Toronto, the Chicago police searched the Englewood Castle, accompanied by a few favored reporters, who enthralled their colleagues a few hours later at Koster's club.

What they found there only confirmed the baffling stories. Past the impressive elegance of the first floor, the public face of the building, the atmosphere turned strange when they toured the upper floors. Hallways did indeed lead to dead ends. Windowless bedroom chambers were soundproofed with asbestos.

The place grew ever more sinister when they descended to the cellar.

Greased chutes, seemingly for laundry, emptied into a basement with no cleaning facilities. Instead, a chemical vat quivered with some kind of acid. There was a powerful kiln, large enough for a person to step into. An operating table stood, set up with medical equipment, but no bed was nearby, nor an elevator to transport a recovering patient. It was a perfect place to dispose of a dead body, so perfect, in fact, that although everything about it was suspicious, and plenty of suggestive evidence was uncovered, no actual proof definitely tied Dr. H. H. Holmes to any murders in the Castle.

Perhaps he was performing illegal operations on fallen women? This seemed like the only logical explanation. For now, all the confounded Chicago law could do was continue the search for the elusive Minnie Williams, and hope the Philadelphia police had enough evidence to convict Holmes of the murder of his partner, Ben Pitezel.

A report surfaced that an offer was made to Holmes to purchase the Englewood Castle, and turn it into a paying museum, and the raucous group at Koster's club placed serious wagers on that.

For the rest of the summer, the newspapers ran wild with stories about H. H. Holmes, making the front pages in cities and small towns across the country. Their readers couldn't get enough lurid details about this mastermind swindler, this murdering fiend. He was a bigamist, and a hypnotist, and a seducer, his numerous women so enthralled by his magnetic charm they stayed loyal despite all evidence of his evil deeds. Reporters obliged the public appetite by fanning out everywhere Henry and Georgiana traveled, from Chicago to Fort Worth, from St. Louis to Toronto to Boston. They interviewed every person they could find with even the slightest memory of the couple.

The public helpfully reported sightings all over the country of the three missing children, of Miss Williams, and of the supposedly dead man, Ben Pitezel, actually alive and well. The children were with their father, disguised as three girls, or as three boys. The children were with Miss Williams, in Cincinnati, in New York, on a boat bound for London. Police struggled in vain to follow up on all the conflicting leads, while rumors spread faster than a cough through a kindergarten.

Reporters showed up at Mary Ellen Ladd's South Side boardinghouse.

"You were a close friend of Miss Yoke's, were you not? Did she tell you anything about her relations with Holmes? Did she tell you her troubles after his crimes were made public? Does she believe in him still?"

Mary Ellen answered them as best she could, describing their friendship at work, the World's Fair visit, and the January errand to the Castle in Englewood. But she shed no light on the marriage.

"Georgiana is not the kind of woman to make those kinds of confidences. I could see it pained her to refer to it, and I thought it best to bury all that happened and ask no questions."

When she went back to her shift at Siegel Cooper the next week, management was not pleased to read the store's name mentioned in the same paragraph as H. H. Holmes. Everyone else buzzed with the excitement of it all, except Harry Chapman, who refrained from his usual after work socializing, and hung back in the cloakroom until he saw her putting on her coat.

"Mrs. Ladd, I'm so sorry you were harassed by the press. Are you all right?"

Mary Ellen now regretted her cooperation.

"Well, my supervisor told me never to speak to a reporter again, and my husband is furious. No man wants to see his wife's name in the paper."

Harry twisted the felt hat in his hand completely out of shape.

"Did they know anything, I mean, did you learn anything about Miss Yoke? About how she is?"

"No, not really. I guess she's in Philadelphia, in seclusion. No one has been able to interview her."

"Are you in touch? Can you write to her?"

"Yes, of course. I can send a letter in care of her mother. It might cheer her up. Will you write to her too?"

"No," he said, "no. It would be an intrusion. You know how proud she is."

Mary Ellen took the hat from his hands, smoothed the fabric, snapped the top up, and gave it back to him.

"I'll send a general greeting, from everyone in the store. So she knows she still has friends. How will that do?"

"That's fine."

"Are you sure you won't write to her yourself?"

"I can't," Harry said. "Not now."

—⊗⊗⊗—

IN THE PHILADELPHIA District Attorney's office, two young clerks clipped articles from newspapers that pertained to upcoming trials. For the H. H. Holmes case, the stacks covered the conference table with cuttings from the Philadelphia papers, and those of Chicago, Toronto, Indianapolis, and any other place reporters might be digging up useful snippets. The office took special care to monitor any rumors or sensational items likely to prejudice a jury.

"What do you have about the woman?" Mr. Barlow asked. "What are they saying about her?"

"A poor victim, distraught with grief, likely broken down for the rest of her life," said one boy, summarizing a long page.

"No, not Mrs. Pitezel, the other one, the Indiana wife. What about her?"

The clerk leafed through the stacks.

"They can't make up their mind," he said, and read few aloud.

"Holmes' Wife on the Way to Him. Holmes' Wife Repudiates Him, Says She'll Knock the Pins Out of His Story. Mrs. Howard Sticks to Holmes. Mrs. Howard Refuses to Talk. Child Bride of Arch Villain In Hiding."

"Well, they must cover their bets," Barlow said. "Does anyone claim she had a hand in it?"

"No, mostly they say that he duped her. But here's one, not too good for our cause. Some neighbor in her mother's town must really dislike her! Listen to this."

Franklin, Ind. — Special. "The circumstances under which Miss Yoke met Dr. Howard are not known here. Miss Yoke is a tall blonde and would have passed as an unusually handsome woman except for her large eyes, which were considered almost a defect. She has a reputation in Columbus, south of here, which is not altogether enviable. Her adventurous tendency may have made her a mark for Howard."

"What, that little bluestocking?" District Attorney Graham reached across the table to read it for himself. "She doesn't even know the time of day."

"Well, we really don't know what sort of girl she is," the clerk said.

"I do. She's an annoying sort."

"I thought she was sweet looking," said the other boy.

"Not to my taste," Graham said. "I like someone more substantial. But it doesn't matter. I just want her to tell the jury Holmes had the opportunity to murder Pitezel, and have them believe her."

Barlow frowned.

"Surely the defense won't try to discredit her, that would be a stupid move."

"No, but the newspapers will make their own verdict."

"It's not helpful, if the jury gets this small-town gossip in their heads. I'd like something more favorable to come out."

"Agreed. Get hold of our contact at the *Inquirer*. Also, find out who runs that Indiana paper."

"What's our offer?"

Graham sighed.

"An exclusive with Frank Geyer."

The reporters were thrilled.

Frank Geyer was the hero whose name was on everyone's lips after the discovery of the dead Pitezel girls. His relentless determination to find them or their bodies, in the face of nearly impossible odds, was universally applauded. He gave generous credit to the help he received from both the public and the press, which further endeared him to everyone.

It was privately whispered, too, among law enforcement circles, that his zeal was partly the result of a personal tragedy, the deaths of his wife and child in a fire.

So with ready pencils, the favored group eagerly waited for the scoop, and they weren't disappointed.

July 30, 1895
TO MURDER WIFE AND MOTHER
Some Startling Evidence Discovered Against Holmes

Indianapolis, Ind. – (Special)—Detective Geyer, who is here searching for the house in which he thinks Holmes murdered Howard Pitezel and disposed of the body, made the startling announcement today that he had discovered enough evidence here to convince him that the arch murderer had laid his plans to murder his wife, Georgiana Howard, and her mother, Mrs. Yoke, in this city as soon as he should get rid of the Pitezel family. Detective Geyer obtained his clue at the real estate office of John L. Wright, who had dealings with Holmes while the latter was darting from one hotel to another with the Pitezel children.

At that time Holmes had been given authority by Georgiana Howard to make a deal with other heirs for her property at Franklin, and had her mother's consent. Detective Geyer asserts that as soon as Holmes had got the few thousand dollars coming to his wife he would have disposed of both Georgiana and her mother as he did of the Pitezels.

IT WAS AN oddly familiar feeling, to be sitting alone once again, staring out of a train window.

Georgiana wore a discreet mourning dress on the journey, and a hat that covered her face with a dark veil, in the hope of being left alone. But in the Indianapolis station, when she went to the telegraph office to notify Mr. Graham of her scheduled arrival, she had to lift the veil, and was spotted by the waiting reporters.

"Mrs. Howard! Just a moment! One word!"

She covered her face, gathered her skirt and ran.

In all the previous year traveling across the country, she never experienced motion sickness before, but now, as she boarded the train to Philadelphia, she felt faint from the heat, and had to ask the conductor to bring her some water. Grasping the cup with two shaking hands and spilling some, she tried to calm her pounding heart with deep, difficult breaths. Her stomach felt like it was in a continuous descent on the great Ferris wheel.

The Indianapolis press had telegraphed their Philadelphia colleagues, letting them know which train she was on, and the word leaked out to the public.

"There she is!" a voice cried as soon as she stepped on the platform, and the next thing she knew she was beset, pressed in by men and women alike, a swarming blur, spraying her with frantic questions.

"Miss Yoke! Mrs. Howard! Is Graham paying you? Will you stick by Holmes? Where is Minnie Williams? Did Holmes hypnotize you? Please! Miss Yoke, give us a word! Just yes or no," and then the people in the crowd were touching her, pulling at her arm and grasping her shoulder. She felt a prod on her hat, and a sharp peck at her hair, and heard a gleeful crow.

"Look! I got a keepsake!"

The dark veil fell sideways as a woman made off with her hatpin, holding the trophy high in the air. There was clapping, and someone in the crowd whistled.

"Hey there, you! Get back, get back!"

The blessed voice of her rescuers, two uniformed ambassadors from Mr. Graham, dispersed the crowd. They stamped through, and took possession of her arms, just before her knees gave out. She crouched between the officers, fingers pressed to her quivering head as they ushered her into a cab.

Half an hour later, it rolled past a high iron gate and up a long driveway.

They brought her to the door of a large brown-brick house, stately and secure. Inside, deep carpet and layers of thick drapery produced a peaceful hush.

"Steady, this way up," a man's low voice directed them, and she was half carried up a long curved staircase. A soothing female presence somehow got her into a nightgown and under soft bedcovers. A hot water bottle was pressed on her ribs. A white haired man appeared, holding a small cup.

"Just a little sip, then you'll sleep," and since she had nothing to lose, she obeyed.

Her refuge was the home of a prominent Philadelphia builder, a longtime friend of the District Attorney. His wife and son were traveling in Europe, so only he, his daughter and the servants were available to look after this unusual houseguest. The daughter was three years younger than Georgiana, the fiancé of one of Mr. Graham's law students. A kind-hearted girl, Jenny McCarr took immediate pity on Georgiana. Caring for her would not only be the work of a Good Samaritan, she determined, but would provide an excellent distraction from her rather boring round of summer house parties and charity work.

There was only one aspect of the project that chafed. Here she was, with the single most famous woman in America, nearly delirious, sleeping in their own guest bedroom, and she was absolutely, strictly forbidden to share the news with even one of her friends.

Mr. Barlow was shocked when a professional nurse admitted him to the room where Georgiana rested. She was dressed, but lying on the bed, leaning against a pile of pillows. A damp cloth covered her eyes, and when she removed it, he had to compose his face.

Her eyes were wide and staring, protuberant, giving her face an expression of continuous shock. When she blinked or tried to close them, the lids stretched smooth, barely able to cover the surface of the eyeball.

She clenched with pain when she moved to sit up. A galloping pulse throbbed on her neck.

He pulled over a chair near the bed.

"I'm very sorry, Miss Georgiana."

"You believe he did it?" Her lips were cracked and white. "The murders in Toronto?"

He nodded his head.

"Why? Why kill those children?"

The nurse poured her out a glass of water.

"We're guessing they knew too much," he said. "They became a danger, and a burden. We're only now putting it all together. We know Henry got the Pitezels, Carrie and Ben, to take part in an insurance swindle. She confessed, told us all about it. They would fake Ben's death, substitute another body, and split the money. Only the swindle was also on them. He always intended to murder Ben Pitezel, I'm sure of that."

The nurse took the glass back from her patient's trembling hand, and set it on the table. She moved to a chair across the room.

"But what did the children have to do with it?"

"They needed a relative to testify to the insurance people that it was really Ben. Carrie was sick, the oldest girl had to stay with her to care for the baby. So Holmes persuaded her to let the middle daughter, Alice, go to Philadelphia with the lawyer, Jeptha Howe, and falsely identify the body. They coached her on what to say. The face was disfigured so she would never know it really *was* her father.

"They got the money. He told Carrie that Alice was on her way to join Ben, who was in hiding, and she might as well send Nellie and Howard along, to keep company with Alice. As soon as Carrie was better, they were all to be reunited, collect their share of the insurance money, start over somewhere new and live happily ever after."

"Insane," Georgiana murmured. "He must be insane. But how can that be? He acts and talks like a normal person."

"He does," Barlow agreed. "*Better* than normal."

"How did Mr. Geyer find the girls?" She hadn't been able to bring herself to read the full account in the newspaper.

"The children wrote letters home, which he was to post for them, and of course he didn't. But for some reason, he kept them, we found them, and between those and the dates and hotel names in your journal, we traced their movements, from place to place, exactly in tandem with your travels last fall. When Carrie was better, he started moving her around too, with each leg of the journey a promise that she would see the children, and Ben, as soon as it was safe. Of course, he was going to kill her, too."

"So the boy?"

"Dead, I'm sure, we don't know where. He was separated from the girls. Mr. Geyer thinks it was near the time he tried to purchase a house in Indianapolis from Mr. Wright. Can you remember anything from around last October that would help him?"

Georgiana thought back to the day they looked at houses, to the thwarted deal at the title company, and Henry's anger.

"No," she said. "I'm sorry, I don't. He went off, whenever he needed to, always for business, I never knew where."

"He claims the children were given to Miss Williams, and that she, in company with some invention named Mr. Hatch, are the ones that killed them. He might as well call him Mr. Hyde! Of course, there's no such person. It's all lies. He's led the police on a merry chase all over the country and across to Europe looking for Miss Williams. We think she hasn't been seen since the fall of 1893, when she signed over her Fort Worth deed."

"*Her* Fort Worth deed?"

"Oh yes, it all belonged to her. When she signed over that deed, I think she signed her own death warrant."

"So the ranch in Texas didn't belong to his uncle?"

"He had no uncle. There never was any uncle, or any ranch. There were never any squatters, or mysterious enemies. There was only the property he and Pitezel stole from Minnie Williams."

"All the time, he said he was selling a copying machine—"

"Actually, that's the only thing that's true. We've seen the plans, and our experts say it's a very good invention. If only he was content with an honest life, with all his talents, he could have been a wealthy man, a legitimately wealthy man. What a waste."

"So the business in Germany was real?"

"No, only the machine. He didn't have a partner there, or a factory."

"But he had postcards, letters with German stamps on them . . ."

"All of which he could have purchased from the Germany exhibit at the World's Fair."

She drew a deep, quivery breath.

"Mr. Barlow, do you agree with what Mr. Geyer said? Do you think he meant to kill my family, or me?"

The nurse's eyes were wide with shock. She shook her head at Mr. Barlow.

"I cannot answer that," he said. "It's curious to me, he never did violence to the two women who had his children, Clara, back in New Hampshire, and Myrtle, the woman in Wilmette. Yet, wherever else he went, young women tended to vanish. Now, supposing you made it all the way to Germany, what would have happened then? You know his ways, how he made up excuses and lies. He lured you there with the promise of this big manufacturing business. But again, there was no partner. There was no factory. How would he have explained that away? What would have been easier, to come up with a good enough story for you, or to make you disappear?"

She pressed the cloth back over her eyes. The nurse stood up.

"I think that's enough for today."

"He wants to see you," Mr. Barlow said.

Georgiana was sitting up now, looking better after two days of rest, but the nurse still hovered behind her chair, giving the lawman a suspicious eye.

"Must I? It's frightening," she said. The thought of talking to Henry made her whole body quake.

"We'd like to know what he wants, what he says to you. It would help us prepare."

Despite her weakened state, Georgiana maintained a bit of her orneriness.

"You could just put him in the sweatbox, like they did to that poor Mrs. Quinlan," she said.

"Really, Miss Georgiana. I don't know what the Chicago police got up to, but I assure you, here in Philadelphia we have no need of those tactics! Where did you hear of such a thing?"

"A woman," she went on, as if she didn't hear him. "A woman, in a sweatbox! It's barbaric. Think of how frightened she must have been," and she shivered, imagining oppressive darkness and parched throat, soaking wet hair and skin and clothes, locked in a space tight as an upright coffin. "The police should be ashamed of themselves."

"Mrs. Quinlan confessed to helping him, she impersonated Minnie Williams, to transfer the deed to the property. Surely you don't excuse that?"

She didn't answer.

"I guess they use that method when someone won't talk," Barlow said. "That's not our problem with Holmes. With him, we can't get him to shut up. He talks all the time. He's even writing a book about himself, did you know that? He's calling it '*Holmes' Own Story.*' Yes, he really is."

Georgiana shook her head.

"Nothing should surprise me now, I guess."

"Unfortunately, whether in speech or in print, every word that comes out of the man is a lie. He lies even when he doesn't have to, he just can't seem to help it. I believe he lies to himself in his sleep," and with this he managed to coax a faint smile out of her.

"So you'll come."

"All right, if I must. Just as long as I'm never alone with him."

Almost to make her fears seem ungracious, Henry showed nothing but concern for her at their meeting. He looked thinner, and pale, but, as always, well dressed and immaculately groomed. He acted the perfect gentleman, trying to get her to sit, and be comfortable, as if, instead of being a prisoner, brought under guard to the prison office, he had invited them all for the weekend to his home in the country.

"Are they treating you well? Do you need anything? I'll tell Shoemaker to get some money from the bank for you," he said, trying to meet her eyes.

It seemed impolite, somehow, to mention the fact that he was here because of cold-blooded murder, as though such a suggestion would wound his delicate feelings. What if she asked him, to his face, "Would you have killed me? My mother? My brother? Did I mean anything to you? Have you any human feelings at all?"

But she didn't. Nothing would come of it. He would find some way to deflect the accusation, astonished, wounded. He truly was what Mr. Graham called him, an endless and infinite liar. She felt sick, exhausted by this absurd charade.

"No," she said, looking at the floor, "no, I want nothing from you."

———

TOWARDS THE END of August, Detective Geyer walked through the cornstalk path and knocked on Mary Yoke's door. In a final attempt to find the body of Howard Pitezel, he placed announcements in all the Indianapolis area newspapers of a renewal of the search, asking for anyone to come forward who may have rented a house or room to a man of Holmes' description, with a young boy, the previous October. The public was so wonderfully cooperative that he had hundreds of leads to follow. To narrow them down to a manageable number, he decided to try once more to retrace his steps and figure out what else Holmes was up to during that fateful month.

He found her kitchen a restful place, after weeks of this exhausting, discouraging search. Mary felt glad for some company, with Georgiana in Philadelphia and Johnny working out at the farm for the summer. By this, his third visit to her home, she didn't even have to ask him how he liked his tea.

"Have you seen Georgiana? She only wrote the briefest note to me, to say she arrived safely. I can't help but worry," Mary said as she poured from the steaming kettle.

"I have not, but I'm sure she's well in hand. Mr. Graham's friend has taken charge of her," Geyer replied. "He made sure to place her where she'd have some companionship, and the girl of the house is engaged to a young man in Graham's office. He can be a gruff sort of fellow, Mr. Graham, but he's thoughtful that way."

"Thank you for telling me that. It does help. And I have to congratulate you, though it came as a shock and a blow to us, that you found those little girls. It must have been terrible, though, for you."

"It was a pitiful sight," he agreed. "One never forgets such a thing. And yet, Mrs. Yoke, I slept more peacefully that night than I had all summer, because I felt that justice was that much closer for them."

"I fear for Georgiana's mental state," Mary said. "I think she may feel some special responsibility about those children."

"Why should that be?"

"Well," Mary said, pausing to sip. "I don't suppose you ever happened to hear the story about the fire?"

Frank Geyer frowned slightly, and tightened his grip on his cup. Mary had no way of knowing, of course, that his personal tragedy involved a fire, and he was not a man to share such a thing. He shook his head.

"In her first term teaching, at the Lowell school in Columbus, there was a fire. It was just before Christmas, and she was the only teacher in the building. She smelled smoke, and went to look, and found the school was burning. She ran to get all the children out, had them hide behind the outbuilding to make sure every one was safe, and barely a minute later, the whole roof came down! Sparks and burning pieces were flying everywhere! Well, of course she was credited with saving the whole class, and although I know now she didn't want to remain a teacher, she really did care about the youngsters. She was proud of herself for what she did. She thought of herself, you see, as someone who had *saved* the lives of children. So now, when this happened, it's all changed, and she had to ask herself, if she had done something different, noticed something, said something, perhaps these Pitezel children would still be alive. There are certainly some folks who think so, who blame her. And that's why I fear for her."

Geyer didn't answer right away, but studied her thoughtfully. Mary was only thirty-three when she was widowed, and was still, now in her late forties, a comely woman, despite all her years of hardship. A devoted mother, he thought, deserving of peace.

"I pray she doesn't believe that," he finally replied. "The only thing I can think of to say to Holmes' credit is how completely he kept her in the dark. No one could have foreseen what this man was doing. No one. I have never come up against such a person as Holmes in my entire career. His capacity for evil is matched only by his ability to convince people of his sincerity."

"Why, that is so true! He came in here and tricked us all. Just a little while of hearing him talk, and the next thing you know you're writing out a check!"

"He wanted you to buy a share of a house," Geyer said.

"Yes, and he had me practically begging him to let me do it. But the worst thing, for me, was he wanted to take away Georgiana's share of the farm. It's not just the money, but you can't imagine what that property meant to my husband's family. It's sad for all of them, that it has to be broken up, but so it is. And Henry just couldn't wait to get a hold of it."

"The farm," Geyer repeated.

"Oh yes, it's a little ways away from here, just southeast of the city. My brother-in-law Nelson has a plan to develop the property into homes, you see, so his mother's heirs receive the most value from it. And Henry just wanted to gamble it away!"

"Had he ever been there?"

"I don't know. He couldn't come to my mother-in-law's funeral, and that's the last time I was there."

"Do you think he might have gone out to see it, while he was here last October?"

"I've no idea where he went! He would always come and go, with this business trip or that one. But now that you mention it, he certainly did seem to know all about it."

A few days later, Detective Geyer's hard work paid off. He discovered the remains of Howard Pitezel in a small house in Irvington, just six miles east of the Yoke farm. There was nothing left of the body but incinerated bones, but the man who rented the house recognized photographs of Holmes and Howard. Some toys, which Howard's father purchased at the World's Fair, were left behind in the house, and later, Mrs. Pitezel would have the heavy task of identifying them.

A helpful neighborhood boy, playing detective, found among the ashes some more charred bones and a complete jaw and set of teeth, stuffed up in the basement chimney. When word of that got out, hundreds of people converged on the house, in wagons, on bicycles, on foot. They ransacked the place, looking for clues and souvenirs. The police finally had to order everyone out so they could finish their investigation.

The man who wanted to start the horror museum back in Chicago showed up too, hoping to buy the stove in which Howard was cremated. He was to be disappointed, though, in his ambition to open the Castle to the public. Later in the summer the

Englewood Castle caught on fire, under highly suspicious circumstances, and the whole building was ruined.

Henry was formally charged with the murder of Benjamin Pitezel in mid-September, and his trial was set for the end of October.

Mary Yoke arrived in the middle of that month, just in time for Georgiana's twenty-sixth birthday. She was warmly welcomed into the household that by now had informally adopted her daughter as their own. The mother, the nurse and the hostess all banded together to keep Georgiana from falling into dark wells of melancholy, self-starvation and nervous exhaustion.

Now there was a deadline to work towards, they could put their minds to the practical problem at hand. What, exactly, was the right and proper thing to wear to a murder trial, knowing the whole world would devour the report of it?

Mr. Graham would send for her when she was needed at the court. Until then, she waited at the house while her host attended the proceedings. In the evening, he returned and gave her a summary of what happened, though she learned more from the daily newspaper accounts.

There was plenty to read.

The first day, Henry caused a sensation by dismissing his attorneys, and declaring he would act in his own defense. He proceeded to question potential jurors with a calm and professional demeanor, as if the law had always been his chosen profession, and even the prosecution had to admit the man had nerves of steel.

The District Attorney also caused a ruckus, when he accused Henry of seducing young Alice Pitezel before he murdered her. A witness, the landlady of the hotel, testified that Holmes spent the night alone in the room with the little girl. Georgiana wanted to lay her head on her lap and weep from mortification when she read this, and it was only the stiff structure of her corset that prevented her from doing so right then and there.

In the evening session, there was a contentious exchange between Mr. Graham and Henry regarding Georgiana. Henry argued her testimony should be excluded, since a wife cannot give evidence against her husband.

"Which wife?" Graham responded sarcastically, causing Henry to chivalrously defend her from the implied slur, indignantly demand the right to correspond with her, and angrily accuse the District Attorney's office of suppressing their correspondence. Judge Arnold intervened and allowed Henry to communicate with the witness.

The next day, officers of the court delivered a letter. It was from Henry, in his capacity as his own attorney, addressed to her in his familiar hand. She threw it into the fire without reading it.

On the second day, the prosecution presented medical evidence.

Henry had changed his story several times since his arrest. At first he said the mutilated body belonged to another man, deliberately staged to swindle the insurance company. Later he claimed it was Pitezel, but that he died from an accident. Finally, he settled on the contention that Pitezel committed suicide. The prosecution's expert witness testified this was impossible, that no man could self-administer chloroform, create an explosion, and then arrange his body in the way they found the corpse.

In the evening session, Henry allowed his attorneys to rejoin the case.

On the third day, Carrie Pitezel was the chief witness. She was kept on the stand for hours, explaining, often in barely a whisper, the convoluted plot that she and her husband engaged in with Holmes.

How Holmes betrayed his partner, killing him instead of providing the substitute body. How he induced her to let Alice come with him to Philadelphia to identify her father's body, convincing her all the while that the body so identified was a fake, but disfigured to fool the authorities. How he next persuaded her to entrust him with the other two children, with the promise they would all join her husband on the run, collect their share of the swindle and start over in a new place, free from poverty. How he moved them all from place to place, like hapless tokens in a board game, herself, the oldest girl Dessie and the baby in one group, Alice, Nellie and Howard in the other, never knowing the whole summer they were all traveling the same route as Holmes and his wife.

Everyone in the court, including the judge, wiped their eyes when Mrs. Pitezel spoke of her murdered children, except for Henry, who simply fixed a disinterested gaze on her. He saved his emotional display for the next day.

Georgiana received her notice on Wednesday afternoon that she must appear in court on Thursday. She spent the night of October 30th in prayer. Before falling into uneasy sleep, the irony of the timing occurred to her. The long dreaded appearance would take place on Halloween.

They waited in a small chamber outside the courtroom, Georgiana, Mary, the nurse, and an assistant to Mr. Barlow. The assistant shuttled in and out past the guard by the door. They could just barely make out the sounds from within, voices raised almost to a shout.

"Whatever is happening?" Georgiana finally asked, when the clerk returned to the room. "What's it all about?"

He tried not to look at her.

"It's the same argument they had before, whether you're a competent witness," he said.

"What, are they saying I'm incompetent, like some sort of imbecile?"

"Oh, no ma'am, it's nothing like that. "*Competent witness*" is a legal term. It means not disqualified, on account of your married status. Holmes is saying you're his legal wife, so you can't take the stand against him."

Now his embarrassment was more acute, and he cleared his throat.

"Mr. Graham presented evidence about the woman in Wilmette, and the first wife in New Hampshire, to prove Holmes is not legitimately married to you. Therefore, you are ruled a competent witness. Do you see?"

Oh, yes, she saw. She understood she would be brought in to explain to the jury, the court, the reporters, and the entire world how she traveled across the country for nearly a year, unmarried, with a man who used her like a harlot. Her folly would be fresh in the minds of the audience. Her humiliation would now be complete.

A seat in the front row was reserved for Mary, as well as an empty one next to her for the nurse who accompanied Georgiana through the side door and into the courtroom. Every eye perused her appearance and demeanor. They noted the high velvet trimmed hat and stylish, tightly fitted black dress. Not mourning, which might imply sympathy with the defendant, but just sober and dignified enough for the setting and occasion.

She fought against the shaking of her body, the weakness in her neck muscles that caused a palsy of her whole head, dreading what was about to happen, when she experienced an unexpected surge of strength, the source of which came from Henry himself.

The court's attention now turned to him, as he wept copious tears at the sight of her. He leaned on the railing, his head in his arms, and sobbed openly.

Pencils scribbled furiously, the astonished audience murmured, and the judge banged his gavel for order. Georgiana recognized this obvious manipulation, and with a sense of deep, renewed disgust, she drew a deep breath, and prepared to answer Mr. Graham's questions.

She recounted the stops on their journey throughout the summer, including her hiring of Jeptha Howe to be Henry's lawyer in St. Louis, and then especially that hot day in Philadelphia. Yes, Henry received a visitor the night before, no, she hadn't seen the visitor. Henry left for the whole day, giving him plenty of time to murder Ben Pitezel and set it up to look like an accident. He came home in an excited mood, strangely jumpy, and drenched with sweat. He insisted they leave on the night train, even though she was still sick. He convinced her to lie to the landlady about their next stop.

Sometimes her voice was too weak to be heard, and she had to repeat herself, or the crier called out her words in a loud voice for the benefit of the court recorder.

She thought the ordeal was over when Mr. Graham finished his questions, but she should have known, Henry could not resist this opportunity for a performance. He whispered a hasty conference with his lawyers, and then announced he would question the witness himself.

He tried to make her look at him. She had not met his eyes, once, since entering the room, and she refused to do it now. He used his softest, most intimate voice even as he attempted to shake her testimony. He tried to evoke memories that should have been tender, succeeding only in making her sick with shame. She whispered her answers to his questions, fixing her eyes on a small knothole in the wooden rail of the witness stand, and concentrated on it with all her might.

She refused to look at him.

She did not look, even once.

Finally it was over. She was dismissed. A man's hand took her elbow, leading her down from the witness stand. She faltered a little on the step, stumbled towards the first row, and fell into her mother's arms.

—∘∘∘—

ALTHOUGH THE PRESS was fixed on the spectacle of Georgiana's testimony and Henry's dramatic sobs, an event more important to the outcome of the trial took place after her turn was done.

"What is this all about, Father?" Jenny asked the next morning at breakfast. She waved a page of the morning newspaper at him. "They say this ruling is a blow for the prosecution."

William McCarr set down his coffee cup.

"Judge Arnold was as sickened by Holmes as anyone, but he is the most scrupulously fair judge there could be, far better than the fiend deserves. He won't allow any witnesses to testify about the search for the murdered children. He rules it isn't relevant to the murder of Pitezel. It means all these people they brought in from all over the country, at least a couple dozen, it seems, including Detective Geyer, can't speak."

"Oh no! Is there a chance he won't be found guilty? Is that possible?"

"The odds makers are saying it's an even bet, after this ruling," but he cut off as Georgiana entered the dining room, and rose from his chair.

"My dear," he said, carefully seating her, as his daughter hurried to the sideboard, filling plate and coffee cup to set before her, and they both looked with worry at her face. She was, in fact, feeling lighter, much better now that her role was over.

"I'm all right," she said. "Mother is still sleeping, poor thing, she was up very late."

There was no point in avoiding the subject of what kept Mary awake. The morning newspapers were spread out over half the long table.

"TEARS DIM HOLMES' EYES" pronounced the headline. Georgiana wrinkled her nose and resolutely took a bite of toast.

"Well, here's some good news, Georgiana," Jenny said. "The drawing of you is so bad, no one will ever recognize you!" She handed the offending page over.

It was true. Her face was rendered long and homely, with heavy lidded eyes so nearly closed she looked asleep, or in a trance. The lines of her lovely dress were roughly drawn, obscuring the shape of the neckline and shoulders, while the outline of the new hat swirled like a lopsided tornado above a flat witch's brim. This final insult on top of injury was so absurd, she could only laugh.

"Mercy, what did I ever do to them?" she said, and passed it over to her host. He glanced at it, at her, then back to the paper again, and shook his head.

"Clearly, the regular court artist was out sick, and they had to pull in a sorry substitute," he said.

"Although," he added, "this likeness of Mike Arnold is not too bad. The one of him in the *Ledger* was so good, at first I thought it was a photograph."

"A photograph of a real person, printed in a newspaper? Can they do that?"

"Oh, my word, yes, Miss Georgiana. Some of them already use photography in advertisements. You cannot imagine all the new inventions just around the corner. I heard the other day, they've figured out a way to send photographs over the telegraph wires, don't ask me how. Before long, I should think all the pictures in the paper will be photographs, and this poor fellow," he gestured at the picture on the table, "will need a new line of work."

"I didn't mean in a technical sense," she said. "I mean in a legal one. Could they take a photograph of you, or obtain one from somewhere, and print it up, just like that, without your permission?"

Mr. McCarr, who was also a political man, gave a sigh.

"Once in the public eye, sad to say, there are few limits of what they may do, if you're deemed newsworthy. So yes, I'm afraid, whether a drawing, or a photograph, if they want to portray you, it makes no difference."

Georgiana was silent for a while, pondering this fresh awfulness.

"I wouldn't be able to go anywhere for a long time, once they printed my photograph," she said. "Not back to Chicago, or Denver. Toronto, St. Louis, Fort Worth – no matter where I went, someone would always know my face, and tell their friends, and the next thing you know, there would be another mob." She shivered.

"So that's why," Jenny said, "it's just as well the drawing is so bad. But, listen, here's some comfort for your vanity, anyway," and, holding the paper aloft, she gave a dramatic reading.

"Every heart went out to her . . . Hers was a face and form well calculated to win sympathy. Slender, delicate, refined, she looked the picture of tender innocence. Her cheeks were flushed, but the rosy tint was becoming; it well set off the head of flaxen hair. Her dainty lips twitched nervously. Her dreamy eyes were downcast . . ."

Georgiana scoffed. "It sounds as if I was there to sell complexion cream. What rubbish! To scribble such nonsense, in such a circumstance, they should all be ashamed of themselves."

"Look over here, Georgiana, I want to see your dreamy eyes!"

"Shame is not something the press is overly supplied with, yet we are stuck with them, and people believe them," Mr. McCarr said. "That is why it's so important to work with them, and not make enemies. When the trial is finished, you'll need to be prepared. Have you worked on your statement yet?"

"My what?"

"You will have to make a statement, after the trial, just a few brief words."

"No. I won't. Why should I?"

"Because you don't want to leave them with the impression you might have something to conceal, or any remaining attachment to

. . . to the defendant. Once it's over, you'll never have to be bothered again. They'll have to write something about you anyway, after all, every story needs an ending, so why not have it be in your own words?"

She had to admit the sense of that, but she adamantly refused to speak in public.

"If I do write something, then Mr. Graham's office can give it out. At least I can get them off my rosy tinted trembling dainty lips!"

Since her part was done, they had only to wait for the end of the trial. Despite the judge's ruling eliminating most of the state's witnesses, the jury had no trouble returning a guilty verdict.

Georgiana wrote a letter to Mr. Graham, enclosing a statement in which she thanked her generous Philadelphia patrons for their kind hospitality to herself and her mother, renounced any and all connection with Henry, and asserted her determination to return to Denver if necessary to legally annul any possible remaining ties to him.

Then she and Mary slipped quietly out of town on a late train, and returned to Franklin, Indiana.

5

RECOVERY

Winter 1895 – Spring 1917

IT WAS A strange sort of letdown, after months of stress and suspense.

The reporters were gone. The neighbors offered a grudging welcome back for Mary, and basically ignored Georgiana.

She ignored them as well, keeping to herself, trying not to wonder who talked to the press about her. She started back at church, but would only slip in with Mary to a rear pew after the service had begun, and steal back out again during the final hymn, leaving her mother alone for the social hour.

Still, it was a sort of calm after the storm.

Mary might have been justified in thinking she had been through, for now, the worst that life could throw at her. So she was utterly unprepared for the next blow, when, just after Christmas, Johnny announced he was quitting high school.

"What? With only five months to go for your diploma? No, out of the question," but he stood firm.

"It's already done. I've talked it over with Uncle Nelson," he said, and this felt like a double sting for Mary. Her brother-in-law conspired with her child to leave home, and here she was, the last to know of it.

"What in the world will you do? How will you live?"

"He's going to advance me my portion of the farm, for tuition to business school," Johnny said. "Grandmother always said we were to use the money for our education, so that's what I'm doing. I'm already accepted, so the diploma doesn't mean a thing."

Mary looked with astonishment at this tall, confident young man, who somehow had snuck in and replaced her scatterbrained little boy.

Even worse, Georgiana unexpectedly took Johnny's side.

"If Uncle Nelson says it's all right, without the diploma, let him go, Mother," she said. She knew full well whose fault this was, and could only imagine the taunting and teasing he had put up with for the past year.

Johnny moved out the next day.

Henry lost his appeal for a new trial. He was condemned to be hanged in the spring of 1896.

In April, he sold a long and rambling confession to the Philadelphia Inquirer, in which he admitted to having what he called his "acquired homicidal mania."

"I am convinced that since my imprisonment I have changed woefully and gruesomely from what I was formerly in feature and figure. My features are assuming a pronounced satanical cast. I believe fully that I am growing to resemble the devil."

He went on to describe, in chronological order, committing the murders of twenty-seven people, including Minnie Williams and her sister, Benjamin Pitezel and the three Pitezel children. A few of the people he named, fortunately, appeared alive and well, proving Mr. Barlow's contention that Henry was utterly incapable of telling the truth, even when he was getting paid to do so.

For the rest of the victims, however, the gruesome details proved true, making Henry the worst, most cold-blooded killer America had ever known. The publicity from the confession revived national interest in the case, and Georgiana felt even more confined to her house.

Everyone was talking, of course, relentlessly gossiping as the execution date approached. Georgiana knew the newspaper men were back, knocking on doors, hanging around shops, engaging in conversations with residents of Franklin, folks who never before in their lives had a reason to speak to reporters.

Even with all of that, she didn't think a simple walk outside the house would be a difficulty, so when she saw the woman, a slight acquaintance, standing in the road with a dog on a leash, she nodded cordially.

That was all it took. The woman jerked the leash and came right to her, not even waiting for a formal hello.

"*You* brought him here," she said.

"I beg your pardon?"

"That man. That killer. *You* brought him into town."

Georgiana swallowed, held her temper, tried to explain.

"I'm sorry. I didn't know he was bad," she said.

"How could you not? You were with him every day!"

"I just didn't. I believed what he said. I never questioned him."

"You never questioned *yourself*."

The woman's words were like spit.

"He was a mesmerizer!" Georgiana almost shouted in protest, but she could tell she sounded guilty, even as she said it. "He was an actor. He could make people believe in him."

"No child in this town was safe, whenever he was here. He might have gone for any of them! How do you like *that* on your conscience?"

With a triumphant snap of the leash, the woman marched away.

Then a messenger delivered a package to the house, and when Georgiana opened it she screamed.

It was a contrite farewell letter from Henry, containing cash, a very large amount, some of the proceeds from the sale of his story.

"Oh! Will he never leave me alone!" she cried, and fell into a panic. She paced the house with the money in her hand, holding it out as if it might sear her skin, looking for a place to hide it. She stuffed it in a bag and shoved it deep in the flour bin, then shook it out and hid it behind some books. Finally she put it in a cookie jar, and placed the jar high up on a top shelf in the kitchen.

Mary called for Uncle Drake and Uncle Nelson. The money, and everything else Henry ever gave her, the pearl locket, rings and other trinkets, the Bible, and the diamond earrings, were gathered up and spread out on the kitchen table, like a pirate's treasure.

"I don't want any of it, you have to get rid of it, tear it up," Georgiana said, and shut herself in the bedroom.

"You can't destroy money, that's against the law," Uncle Drake declared.

"That's right," Mary said. "Someone could use it, and these things could be sold, and the proceeds given to charity."

Nelson fingered the diamonds.

"Does she have a receipt for these?"

"No, certainly not, just the box they came in."

"A respectable jeweler might want to see a receipt," he said. "It would be foolish to take them to a pawnshop, I bet they're worth more than her share of the farm."

"You know, some of his business was honest, isn't that right? He got rent from tenants, just like a regular landlord. So part of the money is fairly hers," Uncle Drake said.

"There's no way to know which part," Mary said.

"I think Nelson should take these earrings to the bank," Uncle Drake argued. "Just put them in a safety box there, and you can forget about them. But later, if she's ever in a fix, and must have ready cash, well, they *are* hers. She deserves something, after all this."

Mary reluctantly agreed to this plan, and tore out the inscription page from the Bible. On the following Sunday, she dropped the Bible and the other pieces of jewelry in the missionary barrel. Nelson opened an account in Georgiana's name at the bank in Indianapolis, and had the earrings locked away. Uncle Drake conferred with Aunt Nan, and then mailed the cash, anonymously, to the Women's Christian Temperance Union in Evanston, Illinois.

A week later, when Mary was ill with a cold, it fell to Georgiana to make the daily walk to the post office. She set forth bravely, defiantly meeting the eyes of everyone she passed, nodding and even forcing a slight smile.

Ascending the steps of the post office, she noticed a good-looking, lanky young man, a bit older than Johnny, hatless and smoking a cigarette, lounging around the sidewalk. He seemed to be watching her, and earned a frown for his trouble.

He was still there when she emerged, letters in hand, and to her amazement, he stepped forward and spoke to her.

"Oh, Miss Yoke, hello there! I'm from the Franklin Democrat. I was hoping for a word. Our readers, Miss Yoke, have contacted us, flooded us, actually, for news of you. That is, how you are. Folks around here are very concerned. They want to know, are you well? How are you holding up? Won't you give us a little statement as to your health just now?"

Georgiana stared at him. He had put out the cigarette and found a rumpled hat, but his slicked hair and forward manners all added to her irritation. She should have ignored him, she knew, but her anger made an answer irresistible.

"Anyone who knows us, or cares for us, knows that they have only to contact our minister, to be reassured as to the welfare of our

— 180 —

family. I gave a statement to the press in Philadelphia, and beyond that I have nothing more to say."

"But we are your hometown paper! Surely you can give another statement for us," he wheedled.

"Actually, you're not," she answered. "I grew up in Edinburgh."

"Ah," he said, and magically, a pad appeared, and a pencil was pulled from behind his ear. "How do the folks in Edinburgh feel about all this? Do they stand by you?"

She started to walk past, her fury should have been evident, but the fool actually grabbed her arm, and forced her to look at him.

"Miss Yoke, our paper is willing to offer a pretty penny, a very pretty penny, for an interview with you. Just a few minutes of your time, and we'll make it worth your while. You should consider it, very carefully. Not many people have a chance to make such easy money."

"No."

Unbelievably, he blundered on.

"Miss Yoke, only think! You could provide some security to your mother. Think of all she has suffered, for your sake. Don't you really owe it to her? After all you put her through?"

Georgiana drew a deep breath.

"I would never want to gain from the misfortune of those children. You are very wrong to imagine I might. Please, get out of my way and leave me alone," she said, and began to move around him, but the young man wasn't quite done.

"You were there," he said.

His voice turned low and insinuating.

"You lived with him, when he did all those murders. He did them, and then he came home to you. It must have affected him, as a husband, as a man. That's what they want to know. You lived with him," and the eyes of the boy met hers, knowing, prurient.

To her horror, she not only blushed in her face, but felt her heart start its irrational pounding, her limbs their treacherous shaking.

Her anger overrode all, and words came out of her mouth that she never in her life used before.

"You can go straight to Hell!"

The night before Henry's execution, Georgiana had a nightmare.

She was walking up a steep path to a castle, a hulking burned out ruin, four stories high, with turrets and rows of windows barely visible in the encroaching dark. She saw Henry's back ahead of her.

"Germany at last!" she called out to him, but he walked on, not listening.

The path grew steeper, and now there was rain, coming down hard, rivulets forming in the slippery ruts. She couldn't see through the rain; her hair stuck to her face. Her soft new Italian leather boots were sinking, sucked deep in the mud. Her smart traveling dress was soaking wet, clinging to her skin like the dress of a woman in a sweatbox.

"Where are we going?" she cried, but he kept marching forward, determined, and she screamed at him through the torrential rain, "You never tell me where we're going!"

He reached a hand back to her, and turned, and when she saw his blank and pitiless face, brilliant diamonds glittered from his ears. He pushed her arm away, hard, and she was falling, tumbling backwards and down, no longer down the steep hill but falling over the side of a boat, dropping down, down, towards freezing black water, and her eyes shot open.

Shivering, teeth chattering, she wrapped herself tightly in her blanket, and didn't sleep again until there was daylight in the room.

When she woke for the second time, it was late afternoon. She sat at the table and sipped some tea with shaking hands. The clock on the shelf told the story.

Henry must be dead by now.

Henry, not she, had been dropped into a pit of darkness.

Henry was gone forever, and she lived, and with his death came freedom. Her task now was to forget, to bury this horrible memory forever.

She looked at the newspaper on the table. And then saw her name.

MISS YOKE'S GRIEF

She took it up and was reading when Mary came in, and she read it again, aloud, in disbelief.

Franklin, Ind. May 8 — Georgiana Yoke, the latest wife of H. H. Holmes, who was hanged in Philadelphia today, is prostrated with grief at the residence of her mother, in this city, over today's occurrence. The blinds of the house were tightly drawn all day, and the general public excluded, but friends from her bedside say her condition is pitiful. Letters are in transit from Holmes to Miss Yoke, it is thought that he has made a confession in them to her. She will wear widow's mourning.

"That boy! That one from the newspaper, I knew he would get at me!"

She was sure of it. It had to be him, telling his boss that he spoke to her, making use of her, for this evil, indecent story. She balled up the paper and threw it at the fireplace, and for the second time in a week, an unladylike oath passed her lips.

LATER THAT SUMMER, Mary planned a little dinner party, hoping to cheer up Georgiana, who had grown listless and quiet, and was not eating properly at all.

Uncle Nelson arrived early, bearing a heavy gift from the farm smokehouse, carried with some difficulty on the train.

Aunt Nan and Uncle Drake were next. The women departed to the kitchen, while the men worked on small household repairs until early evening. When the pork roast and sweet peas and yeast rolls were hot, the other guests, the minister and his wife, appeared, blessing the meal and helping make a brave show of normalcy.

Uncle Nelson entertained them with a war story, which, even in a temperance household, most everyone found funny.

"Our chaplain was the sweetest old fellow in the world, but innocent as a lamb. 'Liquor has never passed my lips, and never will,' he declared. He didn't count on the mischief of those boys, who took that as a gauntlet thrown down. Well, we were down in Kentucky, and it was easy to acquire the main product of that region. The boys got hold of some brown whiskey, and replaced the vinegar in his cruet with it, and they all watched while he ate his salad. 'You know, said he, 'I've eaten greens all my life, and it's amazing how the taste varies from one region to the next. This is the finest salad I've ever had!" Mary shook her head at this, and Georgiana just sighed.

It was during sugar cream pie and tea that the unnamed subject was finally brought out into the open, when the minister turned to Georgiana.

"And how are you getting on now, my dear?" he asked.

"Oh, pretty well, I guess." Noticing the concerned looks of her loved ones around the table, she relented a bit.

"I pray a great deal. I take walks and think, and read to keep occupied, but I'm finding it difficult to put my mind to very much else. It's hard to explain." She picked at the rich dessert with her fork.

"What do you read?"

"Oh, the Bible, of course, and some poetry."

"Poetry, well that's fine. I like a fine, long poem. Tennyson, *Idylls of the King,* that's the sort of one I enjoy," and the minister looked around, inviting other contributions.

Georgiana said, "I've been reading Milton. *Paradise Lost.*"

There was silence as the group thought about this choice, until the minister's wife plunged in.

"What does the poet say to you, Georgiana?"

She thought it over for a moment.

"His words replete with guile,

Into her heart too easy entrance won."

She set down the fork.

"I guess, you know, as a Christian, I always assumed I could recognize evil when I saw it. I thought that for a good person, it would be so obvious, plain as your nose. But, of course, the poem shows how that would be the easy way. Evil is clever. It flatters our vanity, and finds our weaknesses. It can turn anything, even good intentions, to its advantage. Evil is, as the poet said, false and hollow," and she allowed a trace of bitterness in her voice. A little shudder traveled around the table.

"I hope you do not mean to say," the minister hesitated, "I hope you have not suffered spiritually, after this terrible experience?"

Throughout the whole ordeal, a loss of faith was the one thought that never even crossed her mind. She gave the kind man the smile she reserved for people she especially liked.

"Oh, no. God doesn't change. It's only my idea of Man that's different now," she said.

When the meal was over, Mary and Nan stacked dishes to finish later. The night was fine and everyone but Georgiana and Uncle Nelson went for a walk.

They pulled two chairs out the front door so they could sit quietly for a while and watch the lightning bugs, sparking between the cornstalks.

At length Nelson said, "Well, Georgiana, I'm afraid there's been a delay in settling your grandmother's estate. It may take some time longer to get you your money."

"I remember, in Philadelphia, Mother brought some documents to sign, but I didn't pay attention then. Is there a quarrel?"

"Not really, it's only that George feels the portion of the property nearest the railroad tracks is worth less than the lots to the east. The probate court has to figure out the values, and reapportion everything. It's complicated, with so many heirs. It will just take a while, that's all."

"That's too bad, and hard on you, it must take so much of your time."

"No more than my duty," Nelson said, "but I tell you what, the trust can advance you some of your portion, just like we did for Johnny. In case you feel you need it now. I would guess you are thinking of new plans. Have you decided what you want to do next?"

"I think about it all the time," she said. "I think night and day about how I shall escape out of Franklin, but where to go next is still an enigma."

"Escape? Is it so bad to have a secure home with a caring mother? That seems a little ungrateful to me."

"They are not nice to me here!"

Now she let months of stopped resentment burst out.

"They avoid my eye, cross the street when they see me coming. People will hardly speak to me, even at church, and they're not much better towards Mother. But all last year, it seems they couldn't talk enough *about* us. I'm sure they still do behind my back."

"I don't think it's the folks in Franklin so much," Nelson said. "I think it's just human nature. People are much the same everywhere. They get excited when something extraordinary happens, and push away whatever seems frightening. Perhaps some of what you think is meanness, may be embarrassment instead. They don't know what to say to you, so they say nothing at all. Can you consider that possibility?"

"No," she said, and Nelson sighed at her stubbornness.

"Very well, then, back to my question. What shall you do instead?"

"It was so good and generous of Grandmother Isabelle to take care of all of us," Georgiana said, "so I don't want to sound ungrateful. But the problem is, even if my share yields a thousand dollars or more, I still need to work. I can't just spend it down to live on. But invested, it wouldn't bring enough income to move away from here. I have to support Mother."

"Well, then, you're just back to where you were before this all happened, but with the advantage of some savings in the bank," he said. "You'll just have to start over again."

"But what kind of work could I get now? Who would take me? Not another school, certainly. Uncle Nelson, you know as well as I do *you* wouldn't hire me in *your* school!"

Nelson thought of his student's parents, and had to concede her point. No principal in America would hire a teacher with her notoriety.

"I can't work a typewriter, I don't know shorthand. I would go mad at a telephone switchboard. I can't go back to the store. The police and the reporters interviewed all my friends there, and my boss as well. I'd be ashamed to show my face anywhere on State Street. Even if I went to another store, they'd know my name. And besides, I get too tired, when my condition acts up. I can't be on my feet that long. So, let me see." She ticked off the possibilities on her fingers. "I can't sing, or dance, or act, or play the piano, so never fear, I won't go on the stage. I get ill from the sight of blood in a roast beef, so I'd make a pretty terrible nurse. Clearly, the only thing left for me is to learn to juggle, and go on the Chautauqua performance circuit!

"The fact is, I've lost everything, my career, my reputation, my future. He took everything . . ." she trailed off, after alluding to the most awkward subject of all, and Nelson cleared his throat.

"You lost a great deal, Georgiana," he said, "I do not minimize that. But let's just take a moment, and consider what is left to you."

She was silent.

"First, you still have your life, and for that I thank God every day. I imagine what might have been, if that detective, Mr. Geyer, was right, and you and Mary, and Johnny, were all in danger! I feel sick whenever I think of it."

She still said nothing.

"Next, you have your education, which is never wasted, even if you don't use it as you first intended."

Here was a gentle rebuke, a reminder that she walked away from her teaching career, long before Henry made it impossible for her to return to it. She leaned down and tightened the lace of her shoe.

"Then you have your health, and despite the challenges that are yours to bear, you do not suffer from great pain or disability. You still have your youth. You are intelligent. You are faithful. You have a desire to make the world a better place. And," his eyes twinkled a bit, "you have a wonderful family."

"By your lights, I'm the most eligible girl in the world, and that might be so, but for one thing. No man in his right mind will ever want to marry me, after what happened."

Nelson leaned back in his chair, lacing his hands behind his head, and studied the fresh stars now visible over the tops of the trees and buildings across the street.

"We have a situation with some of our female students," he said, apparently changing the subject. "It causes lengthy discussion in the staff lunch room. We'll have a girl, we've known in the school system for years, since she was eight or nine years old, happy and eager to learn and content with her friends. Suddenly, at thirteen or fourteen or so, all is changed. The happy child we knew is now distraught, and mortified, by any small thing. Now all she thinks of is that she must have the latest dress, the smallest waist, the father with the most influential position, the mother with the great-est number of invitations. If these things don't come to pass, she imagines all is lost, she is a failure compared to her peers, no one will ever even walk out with her."

Georgiana smiled at this, recalling the girlhood rivalries of school days, even in a small pond like Edinburgh.

"So even if the girl succeeds in all these goals," Nelson went on, "how many fellows can be a match to her? The average young man is scared to death of such perfection, and rightfully so! No one wants to live with a constant reminder of his own failings and faults."

"Men may not want perfection," Georgiana said, "but neither do they seek out ruin."

"That is unfair." He righted his chair, and slapped his hands on his knees. "Everyone knows you entered into the marriage in good faith. You swore that under oath. No decent man would hold it against you. If he did, he's not the sort you would want to marry anyway."

"Not every man is as good hearted as you are," she said. "You're not being realistic."

"And you are being unnecessarily hard on yourself, as well as on all potential husbands! Men are really much simpler than you make them out to be. They mostly just want to be comfortable in their own homes. They want someone who will be kind, and appreciate them, and laugh at their jokes. If they may have those things, believe me, they will overlook a great many so-called defects."

He's speaking from his own experience, she thought, and it jarred her to realize how long it had been since his wife Isabelle died, less than a year after the death of her father. She remembered watching Uncle Nelson at Isabelle's funeral. He was holding the baby while his other two little boys clung to his waist and his leg. Later, he stood for hours, soberly greeting every person in the long line of mourners who came to pay their respects to the young mother, only thirty-three years old, taken by consumption.

Had it really been sixteen years since that sad day? He was always the one the family counted on, the first to be notified in times of trouble. Who did he call upon?

"Did you never think about marrying again, Uncle Nelson?"

The question popped out, before she thought to stop it, but he was not offended.

"No," he said. "No, I never did. Our time together was brief, but we were very happy, and the boys, and work, are enough for me." He paused a moment. "There is one more thing, Georgiana, that you should count in your list of advantages."

"What would that be?"

"You have your Hoosier common sense, which tells you that no matter what happens, life goes on, and you must persevere. A plan will come to you. Now, shall we go inside, and say a prayer before I catch the train?"

THE STUDENTS OF Franklin College bustled around the campus, noisy and busy. Girls clustered in groups, laughing, talking, and flirting with the gallant boys who carried their books. Their wool skirts, in bold plaids worn above the shoe tops this fall, swirled across the green, graceful and carefree as the brightly colored leaves drifting down from the trees.

The students never noticed the slightly eccentric figure, hard at work across the street.

Georgiana knelt in the yard, obscured by a row of shriveled cornstalks. She wore a man's work jacket, a large straw hat protecting her face from the midday sun, and an old pair of Uncle Drake's rough work gloves. The gloves were too big, and dirt got in the tops and down under her fingernails, but she needed their thickness to protect her hands from the small scythe she used to cut through the tough stems.

Johnny should be the one doing this, she thought, hacking at the spent plant. But Johnny was gone, starting his career, and she was still stuck at home.

How unfair to think that all last summer people tried to throw money at her. First Henry, then the newspaper, and she couldn't in good conscience take any of it. She and Mary would sit at the kitchen table, paper and pencil and documents spread out before them, figuring every possible combination of proceeds from the farm and the house, but without an income, every idea felt too risky. The fear of making a mistake paralyzed them. A move remained out of reach.

She worked hard as a farmer all morning, resentful and morose, frustrated and bored and lonely, hot and sweaty and thirsty and tired.

She was resting by the fence, stretching out her stiff back muscles, when she spotted a man rounding the corner by Dr. Hall's house. She recognized his funny, loping walk even before she saw his face.

His hat perched crookedly. His arms were full, what with his coat, and a paper that must be a street map, and a large bunch of flowers, already a little droopy from the heat.

Flowers, for her.

He remembered.

This was October 17th, her twenty-seventh birthday.

Of course, naturally, he would come now, when she was filthy and sweaty and got up like a scarecrow. She had to laugh.

Georgiana straightened up, took off the work gloves, and waited for her caller to come through the gate.

"Hello, Harry," she said.

—∞—

Two years later, Harry Chapman and Georgiana Yoke entered the Marion County Clerk's office in great spirits. He, as always, kept up a steady stream of jokes, mainly for the fun of making her shush him.

They waited amicably in line. Harry paid the fee and they started filling out the form, a bored clerk behind a counter asking each of them questions by turn and marking the answers in pen. Age and race, occupation and parent's names, place of birth, each routine fact of their lives duly recorded until the process stopped with a deadly silence from Georgiana, and Harry turned in surprise.

Her abrupt changes in mood rarely bothered him. Even after two years her emotions were still fragile, and he took pride in his ability to coax her from occasional melancholy or fearful panics. But in this benign environment, on a most joyful errand, what set this one off?

"What number marriage is it for the bride?" the clerk repeated. "Is it a first marriage for you both?"

"I cannot say."

The clerk tried to seem uncurious as to why a woman would not know how many times she was married.

"What if a first marriage was never legal?"

"Georgiana, dear, come now. There is no judgment here. They only ask the question as a matter of form, no one cares personally about it. Do they?"

Harry looked meaningfully at the clerk, as one man to another, in the presence of a female dangerously close to weeping.

"Oh no, ma'am," the young man said. "They tally the numbers at the end of the month, to keep track of the rate of divorces and such. No names are attached."

"I will not make a false statement," she said.

Harry put his arm around her shoulder.

"You need not, just leave it blank. Truly, no one will ever care or think of it again," and the clerk nodded.

Fortunately, no one waited behind them in line, overhearing this interesting conversation. The clerk took another look at the maiden name, and a quick second look at her face. He understood now, and would have a fine story to tell later at the family dinner table.

At the moment, however, the task of filling out the form completed, the clerk issued their marriage license. The couple turned to leave, the woman now recovered, holding the arm of the man.

"One moment," the clerk called after them, "what newspapers will receive an announcement of the engagement?"

"None," Georgiana said, and allowed Harry to hold the door open so she could march through it, back stiffly erect and chin held high.

HARRY HELPED HIMSELF to coffee at the big coal stove in the kitchen, a comfortable room in a comfortable farmhouse-style home, right in the heart of Indianapolis. A large lace-curtained window opened to a neatly trimmed backyard, and opposite the window stood a great Hoosier cabinet, taking up the whole wall. The latest model, with every modern feature, Harry had it delivered with great fanfare, in celebration of their first Christmas together.

Of course, it was as much of a gift for Mary as it was for Georgiana. Some men might object to sharing a home with their mother-in-law, but Harry never did. For one thing, his traveling sales job kept him away from home for much of the time, and he didn't want Georgiana alone for long.

And he liked Mary. He respected her for a job well done, and for her steady, industrious nature.

And, she was a great cook.

Even in the years when they did not get along so well, Georgiana and Mary had to prepare meals side-by-side, and they developed a wordless, cooperative efficiency that was a wonder to behold. Harry sat at the table and marveled as they silently chopped, and kneaded, and passed tools back and forth, filling the house with tantalizing smells. When he was finally presented with the product of their labors, he always assured them it was wonderful, and he lived in constant danger of eating too much. He considered the arrangement one of perfect domestic comfort.

So when he heard a cry from Mary behind him he was startled, and he turned, nearly spilling his cup. She held up a newspaper, not the Indianapolis one, but an edition from the previous week that a helpful neighbor mailed from Franklin.

"When does it ever end, Harry?" Mary dropped the paper to the table. "Why do they keep it up? What good does it do them? Can this really help them sell more newspapers?"

He picked it up.

"Just look under the 'Local and Personal' column," she said.

March 31, 1899
Friday's Sentinel mentioned the death of Richard A. Yoke, age forty-nine years. Death was due to consumption. Deceased was an uncle of Georgiana Yoke, wife of H. H. Holmes, who recently moved with her mother from this city to Indianapolis.

Harry sat down and took his mother-in-law's hand.

"They don't even say Georgiana Chapman, they don't even give her that. Just "wife" of the murderer! Anyone reading this would think she was still attached to him. It's all so unfair, Harry, they won't ever let it go!"

"Don't worry about it, dear," he said, surprising her with his calm.

In truth, Harry was not as angry as he should have been. The occasional reminder of Georgiana's misfortune rarely disturbed his tranquility.

After all, he won the war. He married the woman he always wanted. His despised rival was lawfully hanged, and the satisfying vision of Holmes in a black hood, dropped and dangling, never failed to cheer him right up.

"Has she seen this?" he asked, and Mary shook her head.

"The post just came, she's already gone out. There was nothing in the pantry today, and she wanted to do the marketing early. She never wants to look at the Franklin paper anyway."

"That's all right then, she'll probably never know. She's so much better now, it might not even affect her like before," Harry said.

Georgiana's health had improved since their move to the city. The nightmares and sudden panics ended. She regained a healthy weight. She still had occasional attacks of her old condition, but these didn't keep her from a busy schedule of temperance, Chautauqua, mission, and suffrage meetings.

Mary sighed. "But why?" she asked again, and he just shook his head.

"I want it to be over. I just want it to be all over for her," Mary said, and Harry squeezed her hand.

"We'll make it over for her. Don't worry any more. Between us, we'll make sure of it." He smiled at her, and she smiled back, conspirators in a plot for Georgiana's happiness.

They didn't hear her approach until she was already through the back door, looking for help with mesh bags filled with groceries.

"All right, you two, it's too early for my birthday, so no secrets!" she said, and Harry released Mary's hand.

"We were discussing the new Bissels, with electric motors, in case Santa Claus should bring you one next Christmas," he said.

He rose from the table and casually opened the stove door and deposited the newspaper, before kissing her cheek and taking a bag.

"As soon as Mother Yoke put on her new glasses, she noticed all the dust in this place. 'What an embarrassment for the next mission meeting,' she said!"

"Not true, Georgiana, I said no such thing!" Mary protested, laughing at her son-in-law's silliness.

"That's just fine, and if Santa does bring the contraption, he'd better bring an engineer to drive it through the house, for I'd surely cause the thing to explode," Georgiana said, and she set about unloading vegetables.

"Speaking of meetings, don't forget, the mission *is* here next week," Mary said.

"Really? How many ladies will there be?"

"Oh, maybe fifteen, or even twenty."

Harry gazed out the window, imagining the scene, and finished his coffee.

"I shall be in Milwaukee," he said.

———

Monday, May 22, 1917

Indianapolis Star
Society Column

A pretty luncheon was given by Mrs. H. O. Garman at her home 2062 North Meridian Street yesterday, the guests being members of the Vincent Chautauqua Literary and Scientific Club. The honor guests were seated with the hostess at a large table adorned with daisies. The other guests were seated at smaller tables arranged effectively with sweet peas, roses and violets. After the luncheon, Mrs. Ruth Baker Day gave a talk on "Life in Russia."

Visitors to Indianapolis often get a tour of North Meridian Street, their proud hosts admiringly pointing out favorite houses, explaining to the guests what interesting, influential personality lives there. This long, extra wide boulevard bisects the city from its center, and showcases much of what is fine about Indiana.

Each of these structures is unique, some English in design, some American colonial. Many are constructed of local red brick, while others represent the tasteful use of Indiana limestone. Some might be called mansions, but none are gaudy palaces. Set far back from the street on deep broad lawns, it's rare for any gates, walls or hedges to block the houses from public view.

In 1917, within these handsome Meridian walls, city leaders made plans and campaigns, designing schools and colleges, hospitals and churches, roads and sewers and streetlights, balancing needs of the rails with the steady spread of automobiles, anticipating the city's growth at the close of the Great War, as soon as that might be. These were busy people.

While the men (for city officials were always men) devised new paths to progress, the city's women gathered and made plans of their own, in their own way.

Women met in clubs. Dozens of club meetings were announced and reported on each week in the Indianapolis newspaper. One such club was to meet faithfully every month for most of the new century.

The Vincent Chautauqua Literary and Scientific Club was one of hundreds of local assemblies based on the home study course developed by the Chautauqua movement in 1874. Established in 1908, this group performed volunteer work, wrote political position papers, and held monthly book discussions.

The club provided an economical way to keep up one's education, as well as intellectual companionship, friendship and support. Though the reading assignments could be daunting, meeting minutes reveal quite a bit of time was also spent on planning luncheons and other social events, sometimes with great hilarity.

One of these luncheons took place on a Sunday afternoon in May on North Meridian Street. The guests were former members, in town for a visit, as well as associate members under consideration, upon completion of study requirements, for full membership to the club.

Mrs. Laura Gillespie, a longtime member, assisted the hostess, Mrs. Garman, with the arrangements, and now she surveyed the tables with satisfaction. They looked charming and festive, the flowers freshly picked from the Garman's cutting beds. Place cards, fashioned to look like telegrams, were inscribed with clever verses. Whoever thought of that idea would win a round of applause.

Guests arrived, laughing and talking in the foyer, admiring the season's new "mushroom" style hats, comparing plans for the summer. A new woman, an associate whose name escaped Laura, came over to admire the tables with her.

"How lovely everything looks, Mrs. Gillespie!" she exclaimed, causing discomfort for the one whose memory lapsed, so she merely smiled and thanked her companion. Yet the woman lingered.

"I am so looking forward to the club," she said. "I understand you've been a member from the beginning."

"Yes, indeed," Laura said. "I don't know what I should do without meetings to look forward to. Everyone misses them in the summer. When we rejoin in the fall it's just as if we never stopped, the group is so companionable."

"I wonder," the woman said. "I do have some questions, that is, I wonder if you could tell me a little more."

"Why, of course. Certainly, is there something about the readings?"

"Well, no." The woman leaned over the table and straightened a flower. "I wondered something about a member, that is, I wondered if you could tell me something about a member. The fact is," and now she looked directly at Laura, "the fact is I believe you are friends with that lady over there." She nodded towards a table by a tall window overlooking the garden, where a trio of women chatted with great animation. Laura followed her look. It led straight to Mrs. Georgiana Chapman.

Georgiana's stylish hat lay on the table, and through the window the spring sunlight caught her hair, still blond but now touched with silver. At forty-eight, she remained slender, her back perfectly straight. Her pretty face scarcely showed a line. She appeared lively, engrossed in conversation, hands gesturing and voice laughing with the women at her table. Georgiana Chapman looked very happy.

Marriage and motherhood long ago taught Laura the value of taking a deep breath before speaking in anger, and she did so now. After all, it wasn't the first time this happened, and was not really so surprising, even after all these years, that someone might still ask.

"My husband and I have the pleasure of long friendship with Mr. and Mrs. Chapman. Mr. Gillespie and Mr. Chapman are both in the wholesale food trade, you see, and have frequent business contacts, as well as social. Some time back, we traveled with them to visit the Chautauqua resort in Winona, have you seen it? What Brother Sunday has accomplished there is remarkable. We stayed two weeks, very enjoyable. Really, it's a most interesting place," but the questioner would not be put off.

"My neighbor is friendly with Mrs. Chapman's neighbor, Mrs. Pedlow, over on Central Avenue. She was visiting, and talking with some of the other neighbors, and was told the most, really the most extraordinary thing, I could hardly believe it. But I did wonder. Can you tell me, can it be possible, was she really once married to that man, that terrible murderer, back in the nineties?"

The woman waited, slightly flushed, slightly breathless.

"That is true. Georgiana Chapman is the former Miss Yoke."

"Oh my! Oh, my goodness. I remember reading about it when I was at school, no one could talk of anything else for weeks! Well, I mean, how does she bear it? Those children, and everything!"

"She bears it with fortitude."

"Does everyone else here know?"

"Yes, of course. The original members go back a long way, we all know a great deal about each other. But we respect Georgiana too much to ever, ever speak of it. The memory would cause her pain, and we would never want that." She paused. "I'm sure anyone who joins the club as a full member would agree."

"Oh," the woman said, catching her meaning immediately. "Oh, of course, Mrs. Gillespie, I completely understand! Thank you, and don't worry. Say nothing more about it, and neither will I."

"Good," Laura said. "I do hope you enjoy your lunch."

6

EPILOGUE

JOHNNY YOKE FINISHED business school and went to work for the Parry Manufacturing Company in Indianapolis. He played on two amateur baseball teams, the Wonderland Club and the Arcadians. Eventually he realized his dream of working in the automobile business, first at Studebaker, then Maxwell Motor Company, which later became the Chrysler Corporation.

In 1923, he was married and living in Syracuse, New York. Georgiana Chapman and Mary Yoke took the train out east to meet his new young wife, and according to family lore, the visit did not go well. Prohibition was in effect, and liquor was discovered in a kitchen cabinet.

"Why would they blame me? It's your bottle, after all!" Johnny's indignant wife said, after the scolding guests departed.

"Never mind," Johnny said. "There's no pleasing those two. They've always been old fashioned."

There was not a complete estrangement in the family, however. Christmas cards were exchanged every year between the two households.

In the early 1920's, Harry, Georgiana and Mary moved to Los Angeles, but Mary only had a short time to enjoy the warm winters. Three years after the awkward visit to Syracuse, in 1926, she died at the age of eighty.

Harry and Georgiana brought her body back to Indianapolis, to rest by her husband at Crown Hill Cemetery.

She never knew that soon she would have two grandchildren in Syracuse, a boy and a girl. She would have been thrilled to know Johnny's children both went to college. Her grandson, in fact, would go on to earn a Ph.D. in chemistry.

———

HARRY AND GEORGIANA built a cozy home in an up-and-coming neighborhood in Santa Ana, a sweet stucco cottage, in the Tudor Revival style, with multiple, steeply pitched gables and a rounded arch door. An orange tree grew in the front yard.

Every morning Harry picked oranges to squeeze for his breakfast, and when visitors came, no matter what time of day, he always produced a glass of fresh juice for them.

They had a quiet life in California together for more than twenty years. Harry continued in the wholesale food business, thriving in spite of the Depression. Voter rolls show that Georgiana was registered for every election.

———

ON JULY 20, 1945, at the age of 75, Georgiana died from a heart attack. She was buried in Hollywood Cemetery.

A short time later, as instructed in her will, Harry sent some things to her sister-in-law in Syracuse. Among them was a pair of magnificent diamond earrings.

"Where in the world did these come from?" Johnny's wife asked in wonder.

It was a mystery, what such modest and unassuming people would be doing with such ostentatious jewelry. If Johnny knew the answer, he never shared it. Fifty years later, one of his grandchildren happened to read a book about H. H. Holmes called *Depraved*, and only then did the family learn the origin of their diamond earrings, resting in a deposit box at the bank.

In 1959, some members of Johnny's family traveled to California, and they stopped by to pay a call on Harry.

He still lived in the pretty cottage in Santa Ana. Over ninety now, he looked frail, but was well enough to go with them to the cemetery, and leave some flowers at Georgiana's grave.

As they left, he talked to them about her.

She was a wonderful woman, he said, and a wonderful wife. He felt blessed for all the time they had together.

To the end of his days, Harry missed his lovely Georgiana.

Sources and Acknowledgments

A Competent Witness is a work of speculative fiction, closely based on actual events. I invented dialogue and inferred relationships in the interest of telling the story, but tried to portray the lives of real people with truth and respect.

Thanks to my early draft readers and feedback givers:

John Borowski, Sally Erickson, Amy Shannon, Kathy O'Hara, Bob and Noel Kirsch, Elaine Stenzel, Nancy Bishop, Fern Schumer Chapman, Shirley Coleman, Walter Carlson, Debora de Hoyos, Cindy Beckel, Robert Kriss, Laura Schriesheim, Lynne Grenier, and Rita Hoke.

Thanks to my first and best reviewer, my sister Nancy Peterson, and to my patient and supportive family, Leslie Nickels, Lon Berkeley, Dave Becker, my children Jeff and Meredith, and my husband and life coach Doug.

Thanks to my insightful editor, Joe Sharkey.

I was first asked to do research on Georgiana Yoke in 2006 by the Lake Bluff History Museum, and I thank Kathy O'Hara and the Museum for inspiring the project. Special appreciation goes to the Lake Forest Library, for access to their extensive resources, from newspaper and genealogy databases to interlibrary loans of books and microfilm.

My first major resource in discovering Georgiana's history came from the Johnson County Museum in Franklin, Indiana, with the help of their archivist, Linda Talley. She made my interest known to a resident there, Mr. Alan Jones, who provided a wonderful trove of information.

When Alan was a college student in the early 1960's, he became fascinated by Georgiana's story after reading about H. H. Holmes in a true crime anthology. He identified several elderly residents still living in Franklin, who remembered Georgiana and the Yoke family. He interviewed these people and wrote down their recollections. He kept them ever since, along with other documents he collected, such as John Yoke's military medical record, and Mary Yoke's property transfers. On learning someone inquired about Georgiana, he brought the entire file to Linda, who added it to the Museum's existing archives on the Yokes.

Alan kindly took the time to give me a tour of Franklin, pointing out landmarks such as the small triangular lot opposite Franklin College where Mary Yoke's house once stood, and the street corner where a neighbor described watching Georgiana stroll by with Holmes in the fall of 1893, recalling his tall silk hat and gold-topped cane.

Piecing together the story from Georgiana's point of view required reviewing all the major works about Holmes. These must always begin with Frank Geyer's detailed memoir, *The Holmes-Pitezel Case (1896)*, which was reproduced, along with other primary source material, in John Borowski's *The Strange Case of Dr. H. H. Holmes (2005)*. The most recent and well-known depiction is in *The Devil in the White City (2003)* by Erik Larson, but the time period that concerns Georgiana is covered in more detail in Harold Schechter's *Depraved (1999)*, David Franke's *The Torture Doctor (1975)*, and a fictional treatment, Allan Eckert's *The Scarlet Mansion (1985)*. *The Girls of Nightmare House (1955)* by Charles Boswell, with a rather misleading title and pulpy cover art, was basically a history of the trial. Other versions of Holmes' crimes appeared in numerous anthologies, including *The Mainspring of Murder (1958)*, *Chicago Murders (1945)*, and *The Pinkerton Casebook (1940)*.

Newspaper accounts were obviously crucial in researching this story. Newspapers consulted included the following:

Boston Daily Advertiser
Boston Morning Journal
Chicago Daily Tribune
Chicago Herald Tribune
Chicago Inter-Ocean
Columbus Herald
Edinburgh Courier
Franklin Democrat
Galveston Daily News
Indianapolis Morning Star
Milwaukee Sentinel
New York Herald
New York Times
Philadelphia Inquirer
Rocky Mountain News

I thank Northwestern University for allowing access to the *Nineteenth Century Newspapers* database and rare microfilm archives. Thanks to the State of Illinois First Search database grant, which allowed temporary full text access to many other nineteenth century newspapers.

Information about the Yoke family farm came primarily from an undated Indianapolis Times article by Agnes McCullough Hanna, which may be found in the Yoke file of the Indiana State Library Genealogy Room, and from a paper by Carol Hall of the Marion County Historical Society, *"Gently Rolling Hills and Winding Creeks — The History from My Yard."* Thanks to Ms. Hall for making both documents available.

I am indebted to the people working in libraries, museums and historical societies who provided materials and patiently answered my queries, including:

Lycoming County Historical Society
Hendricks County Museum
Danville Public Library
Edinburgh Public Library
Butler University
Franklin College
Crown Hill Cemetery
Indiana Historical Society
Indiana State Library
Marion County Public Library
Columbus Historical Society
Historic Landmarks Foundation of Indiana

Thanks to other interested individuals:

Alice Glover, for providing the abstract of the Yoke farm and the last will and testament of Isabelle Yoke.

Cynthia Ward, for research on the Chapman home in Santa Ana, California.

Torin Scott, owner of the Toner-Maley House Bed and Breakfast, the lovely Italianate mansion built by Mary Yoke's cousin in Edinbugh, Indiana, for her kind hospitality.

Dr. Cheryl Jackson for sharing her knowledge on ophthalmic goiter, which today is called Graves' Disease.

Dr. Carlotta Rottman, for her opinion on John Yoke's chronic skin condition.

Bill Black, for his help with genealogy research.

Finally, I am deeply grateful for the cordial and informative correspondence from the late Mrs. Mary Yoke, the widow of Georgiana's nephew.

Other helpful resources included:

Ancestry.com, Provo, Utah.

Bodenhamer, David. The Main Stem: History and Architecture of North Meridian Street. Historic Landmarks Foundation of Indiana, 1992.

Brown, Robert. The Story of the Central Normal College, 1878-1946. R. A. Brown, 1984.

Bulkley, L. Duncan. Eczema and Its Management. Putnam, 1881.

Bussler, Mark. Expo: Magic of the White City. DVD. Inecom Entertainment, 2005.

Central Normal-Canterbury Association. Central Normal College, 1876-1945. 1985.

De Becker, Gavin. The Gift of Fear. Dell, 1997.

DeWitt, Margaret. The Devil Visits Franklin Indiana. DeWitt & Woodrum, 1998.

De Wit, Win. Louis Sullivan: The Function of Ornament. Chicago Historical Society, 1986.

Diebold, Paul. History and Architecture of Meridian-Kessler. The Meridian-Kessler Neighborhood Association, 2005.

Foster, Vanda. A Visual History of Costume, the Nineteenth Century. Drama Book, 1984.

Hare, Robert. Without Conscience: the Disturbing World of the Psychopaths Among Us. Pocket Books, 1993.

Hiller, Nancy. The Hoosier Cabinet in Kitchen History. Indiana University Press, 2009.

Hogate, Julian. History of Central Normal College. 1939.

Knight, Oliver. Fort Worth: Outpost of the Trinity. University of Oklahoma Press, 1953.

Leach, William. Land of Desire: Merchants, Power and the Rise of a New American Culture. Putnam, 1993.

Marsh, William. I Discover Columbus. Semco Color Press, 1956.

Mattingly, Carol. Well-Tempered Woman: Nineteenth Century Temperance Rhetoric. Southern Illinois University Press, 1998.

Merrill, Samuel. The Seventieth Indiana Volunteer Infantry in the War of the Rebellion. Bowen-Merrill, 1900.

Methodist Hymnal: Official Hymnal of the Methodist Church. Methodist Publishing House, 1932.

Milano, Sarah Smith. Faces Across the Counter: A Social History of Female Department Store Employees 1870-1920. Thesis (Ph. D.) Columbia University, 1982.

Okrent, Daniel. Last Call: The Rise and Fall of Prohibition. Scribner, 2010.

Otto, Sarah. A History of Edinburgh, Indiana. S. B, Otto, 1986.

Page, Tim. What's God Got to Do With It? Robert Ingersoll on Free Thought, Honest Talk and the Separation of Church and State. Steerforth, 2005.

Pirtle, Caleb. Fort Worth, the Civilized West. Continental Heritage Press, 1980.

Rosenberg, Chaim. America at the Fair: Chicago's 1893 World Columbian Exposition. Arcadia, 2008.

Sanders, Leonard. How Fort Worth Became the Texasmost City. Amon Carter Museum of Western Art, 1973.

Selcer, Richard. Hell's Half Acre: The Life and Legend of a Red-Light District. Texas Christian University Press, 1991.

Souvenir Programme of the Dedication Ceremonies of the World's Columbian Exposition, 1892.

St. Romain, Darrel. History of Hymns: Victorian Hymn a Favorite at Funerals. www.umportal.org/article.asp?id=3400, 2008.

Steel, Valerie. The Corset: A Cultural History. Yale University Press, 2001.

Steel, Valerie. Fashion and Eroticism: Ideals of Feminine Beauty from the Victorian Era to the Jazz Age. Oxford University Press, 1985.

Stout, Martha. The Sociopath Next Door: The Ruthless Versus the Rest of Us. Broadway Books, 2005.

Thomas, M. E. Confessions of a Sociopath: A Life Spent Hiding in Plain Sight. Crown, 2013.

Vincent Chautauqua Literary and Scientific Club. Meeting minutes, various dates between 1908-1920. Indiana Historical Society, Indianapolis, IN.

Wend, Lloyd. Give the Lady What She Wants: the Story of Marshall Field & Company. Rand McNally, 1952.

Whitaker, Jan. Service and Style: How the American Department Store Fashioned the Middle Class. St. Martin, 2006.

The Whitechapel Club: Defining Chicago's Newspapermen in the 1890's. American Journalism, 15:1, Winter 1998, pp. 83-102.

Made in the USA
Charleston, SC
29 August 2016